WEEKLY READER

Children's Book Club

Education Center • Columbus 16, Ohio

PRESENTS

FEAR IN THE FOREST

BY CATEAU DE LEEUW

FEAR
IN THE FOREST

BY

CATEAU DE LEEUW

ILLUSTRATED BY LEONARD VOSBURGH

THOMAS NELSON & SONS
NEW YORK

Edinburgh   *Toronto*

BOOKS BY CATEAU DE LEEUW
Fear in the Forest
One Week of Danger
The Dutch East Indies and Philippines
William Tyndale, Martyr for the Bible
WITH ADELE DE LEEUW
Breakneck Betty
Showboat's Coming
The Expandable Browns
Hideaway House
Mickey the Monkey

WEEKLY READER
Children's Book Club
Edition, 1960

© 1960, by Cateau De Leeuw

All rights reserved under International and Pan-American Conventions. Published in New York by Thomas Nelson & Sons and simultaneously in Toronto, Canada, by Thomas Nelson & Sons (Canada), Limited.

Library of Congress Catalog Card Number: 60-7290

Printed in the United States of America
American Book-Stratford Press, Inc., New York

This book is dedicated to the memory of those boys of 1794 who were men and those men who were heroes

FOREWORD

There was only one way to make Ohio territory safe for the settlers, and that was to defeat the Indians. General Harmar had tried it in 1790 and had lost to the savage foe. The following year General St. Clair's troops marched north, only to suffer what was, perhaps, the greatest defeat our army has ever known.

Fear was rampant along the frontier, and the Indians grew bolder day by day. President Washington named Major General Anthony Wayne to accomplish what the two generals had failed to do. Wayne's preparations were so careful and detailed that his nickname of "Mad Anthony" seems out of place here. He drilled his men unmercifully, and taught them to fight the Indians with their own methods. The result was an army that was tough, and obedient to command. When he felt the men were ready to march against the Indians, he went north to Fort Greeneville.

This was in October, 1793. He would have liked to finish the matter once and for all at that time, but he had not enough supplies to back up an army on the move. Until he had them, General Wayne was determined not to attack. This meant a long winter of drilling, and, when spring came, an urgent need for more and more pack-trains to bring food and ammunition to the string of forts he had built right up to the border of the Indian country.

The Indians were assembled in great numbers to oppose him, but Wayne did not give them the chance. He was always secure in his forts. Even on the march, his men had strongly fortified encampments every night. Inevitably, the number of Indians dwindled. Food was scarce for such a large gathering of them. Small bands went off to hunt; some pounced upon the supply trains or settlers' cabins. They made one effort, late in June, to storm Fort Recovery, and were repulsed. After that their force lessened. By the time Wayne met them in battle at Fallen Timbers, on the twentieth of August, 1794, the victory was his within an hour.

But he could not have won that victory without the necessary supplies. The men and boys who drove the pack-horse trains faced real danger to bring the essential rations from Fort Washington. This book, true to the period in action, and giving something of their speech, is meant to tell a little of their thrilling story.

The astonishing tale of the "spies" and their captive, Christopher Miller, is a true one. I have used real names and the descriptions of real places wherever possible, and I am grateful to those pioneers who left behind them the account of their stirring times.

C. De L.

FEAR
IN THE FOREST

CHAPTER ONE

Would the long, hot afternoon never end? Daniel wondered. He wiped the sweat from his forehead and flung back a lock of hair that kept falling forward. The June sun burned on his back. He leaned for a moment on his hoe and looked around.

Jeptha and Luke were visible farther down the field, and the sound of Mr. Worder's axe came from the woods beyond. Little Uzziel, who was too young to do much, was chasing the pigs. Beulah's high singsong voice rose above the sound of the hominy mortar as she called to her sister in the house.

It was a busy scene. It had a homey look, for everyone was working, and they were working for one another as well as for themselves. Only he was separate; only he did not belong in the picture.

His stomach rumbled with hunger. He looked up at the sky but the sun was still high in the heavens; it would be a while till supper.

Milly, the baby, came running from the cabin, her older sister after her. Milly wore a short shift and Elvira caught at it as she ran. Milly thumped to the ground and bellowed in fierce resentment, her face growing redder and redder. Mrs. Worder came from the house and picked her up. She shook her finger at Elvira and went back into the cabin.

Daniel could not make out any of the words, but the sounds of the child's crying and Mrs. Worder's voice had reached him. The figures moved woodenly in the harsh sunlight of the clearing around the cabin. There was no feeling of reality to them.

Daniel suddenly spoke aloud to himself. "Sometimes I don't feel nothin's real any more," he said. And then, ashamed of what lay behind his words, he bent to his work again.

It was much later, when he had stopped thinking about anything except how hungry he was, that he heard a shout from Luke. He looked up and saw a horseman coming out of the woods from the narrow trail that led north to the Indian country, and south to Columbia. It was on that trail, he remembered, that—

"Dan'l!" Mr. Worder's gaunt form had appeared from the woods. "What's the hallooin' for?"

"We got a visitor," Daniel answered. "From the north."

Mr. Worder shouldered his axe and came forward eagerly. "From the north, eh? Might be, he'd have news of Gen'l Wayne and the Legion." He beckoned to the lad to follow him, and Daniel willingly turned from the hot, backbreaking work.

Abel came into view then, with Jonas the ox dragging a crude sledge of logs. "What's up?" he shouted. "Indians comin'?" His laugh had a cruel edge to it, and he faced directly toward Daniel, as if to dare the younger boy to object.

Daniel winced at the words—he couldn't help it. "Indians comin'?" might be said in fun, with the bright sky untouched by cloud or smoke, but Daniel's mind was swept by a black, unreasoning terror.

Mr. Worder shouted back, "Visitor!" and Abel, as eager for news as anyone else on the frontier, called, "Whup gee!" and "Giddap!" He flicked Jonas on the rump with a little leafy switch he carried, anxious to get back to the cabin with the others.

Daniel heard Mrs. Worder saying to the man on horseback, "Lands sakes, yes, it's too far for you to go afore dark. You'd best spend the night here. You're right welcome, I'm sure."

"I had expected I was not more than a few miles from Covalt's station by this time," the stranger said. "I must have been traveling slower than I thought."

"It's not that it's so *far*," Mrs. Worder amended, "but it takes so long. With all the rain we've been havin' it's boggy in spots, and the trail is as good as lost some places."

13

"Well, it is kind of you to offer hospitality," the man said with a slight bow, "and I shall be happy to avail myself of it." He turned to Luke, who was standing openmouthed beside him, staring like a lack-brain. "I'd rather not turn my horse loose tonight. I'm anxious to press on as soon as possible in the morning, and don't want to waste time hunting for him in the woods."

"We got a lean-to for Jonas," Luke said. "I'll put him in there."

Mrs. Worder was issuing orders like a general on the eve of battle. "Elvira, see what you can rustle up in sass. Beulah, get movin' with that hominy. We'll need more. Jeptha, bring in more wood. And you, Daniel"—her voice hardened—"take the gun and see what you can git in the woods. We're short on meat," she added apologetically to the stranger.

Daniel paled. Was the light already failing? Was it still as bright as it had been a few moments before? Or was it only the cloud of fear which had darkened the scene for him?

He saw the others staring at him—some curious, some sneering—as if they wondered what he would do. He took the musket without a word, picked up the powder horn and bullet pouch, and went out. He was not even to know the name of the stranger, he thought angrily, keeping his steps firm and not too fast until he was out of sight.

He wanted to run; he wanted to find his game and shoot it and get back to the cabin in a hurry. But hunting wasn't something you could do in a hurry. He wanted to stay close to the clearing. But he would never be able to find game so close to the cabin. His breath came hard, and the knot of fear grew tighter and tighter in his chest.

14

It was pure luck that showed him the quail, for he was too deep in his thoughts to be much of a woodsman. He grew very still, and loaded the musket with slow movements. He had been foolish not to have loaded it before he got into the woods. Then, just as he was raising it to sight, the quail took alarm and scurried under some leaves.

To his surprise, there was movement in the trees ahead. The quail's panic had communicated an alarm to some other woodland creatures. Daniel's heart lifted. Turkeys! Several of them roosting in the trees! As they started to take flight, he fired, and brought down a big one.

He caught up the feathered body, hardly waiting to make sure that the bird was dead, and started back toward the Worder cabin on the run. But he slowed to a walk as the woods thinned, and tried for nonchalance when he dumped the bird onto the floor just inside the door. "Here's your meat," he said.

"Quite a hunter, aren't you?" the stranger said, smiling at him from the log-stump seat. "I never saw quicker work than that!"

"It never happened afore, neither," Abel said with a snort. "Most times, Dan'l is so busy lookin' for Indians he don't see the game."

"Well, that shows he's a cautious lad," the stranger said. "And heaven knows there have been too many Indians about for comfort these past few months. I'll be glad to get back to Cincinnati."

Mrs. Worder, busy at the fireplace, opened her mouth to ask a question, but her husband was ahead of her. "What were you doin' up north?" he asked.

The stranger sighed. "Being a fool, most likely," he said

with wry humor. "I come from eastern Pennsylvania, and the stories I had heard about the fine land to be had here in Ohio made me itch to get my hands on some."

"You a farmer, Mr. Reese?" Luke asked suddenly.

Daniel thought, So that is the man's name—Mr. Reese!

"No, but I was brought up on a farm, and know good land when I see it. . . . This is a fine place you have, right here," he told Mr. Worder.

Mr. Worder's chest swelled. "Not as rich soil as down towards the river mouth," he said modestly, "but we don't git flooded out every spring, neither."

"I can see that. . . . Well, I decided to come west and investigate for myself. I had a mind to do some investing in land, and then sell off the sections when I got back east. Mr. Symmes' purchase was what got me started, I suppose."

"You going to do it?" Luke asked curiously.

Mr. Reese was silent for a moment. "I—don't know," he said finally. "I did not go as far north as I had planned, for I could see almost at once that there is still too much danger from the Indians in that part of the country."

"Here, too, I reckon," Mr. Worder said glumly. "Dan'l's pa got kilt by the Indians—that's why he's livin' with us."

"But that was three years back, pretty near," Abel said.

"The Indians are still a menace, however," Mr. Reese said. "Even as close to the Ohio River as this. I could not, in all honesty, sell land to people under such circumstances, without warning them of the dangers, and I am very much afraid that if I did that, I would not be able to sell it at all."

"Shucks!" Mr. Worder said. "*We* knew it was sort of dangerous when *we* come, but that didn't stop us."

Daniel's thoughts turned inward then. His father had known the Indians were dangerous when he came out in 1790, and they *had* stopped him. And how many others, he wondered? There were so many stories of killing and scalping, of burning and pillaging, of crops ruined and people starving and homeless. He admired Mr. Reese for his stand. He would, at least, not lure folk out to such unfriendly country without warning them.

Supper was an unusually fine meal, in honor of the unexpected guest. Instead of the usual mush and milk, there was boiled turkey. It was flat, since the Worders had no salt left, and so was the hominy, mixed with dried pumpkin to stretch it. But there was at least a little honey on that. The food was more than welcome to Daniel after his day's work in the sun. There was so little corn left at this season that if the stranger had come a few weeks later there might have been none to give him.

The little cabin was crowded when all were seated at the rough puncheon table, but later, after they had talked before the fire for a while, they would have to make room for Mr. Reese to sleep on the floor. The one bed in the cabin belonged to Mr. and Mrs. Worder, and the three older boys and Daniel slept in the shaky-floored loft above. The girls, Uzziel, and Mr. Reese, would have to fit themselves into the small amount of floor-space left.

The talk after supper was good. Mr. Reese, being lately from the east, had much to tell them of events on the Atlantic seaboard, and he had had an adventure or two in coming through the Pennsylvania mountains. "My trip down the Ohio was completely uneventful, however," he added. "Not an

Indian to be seen; not even a snag in the river to slow us up, and we made the trip riding the crest of the spring freshets in record time."

Mr. Worder said suddenly, "Dan'l's folks were from Pennsylvania. His ma died there, and his pa brought the young-un along with him when he come west to make a new farm. He settled right above us here, not far from the old Miami Indian trail. I reckon that was his big mistake—he was too close to the varmints, and they couldn't resist havin' a try at him."

Mr. Reese said thoughtfully, "Those old Indian trails were well placed for travel, though. It is surprising how they instinctively chose the most desirable routes through the country."

"No need to give them all the credit," Mr. Worder said dryly. "Animals made the trails afore the Indians. Buffalo traces, lots of 'em."

"I kept to the pack-horse trails whenever I could," Mr. Reese said, "although I dislike traveling through strange and dangerous country with no chance to see far on either side of me or to look ahead or behind for any distance."

"I hear Gen'l Wayne's been cuttin' roads right through the forest," Luke said. "Sixty feet wide, we were told, but that don't hardly seem possible."

"It is, though. He has to have plenty of room for the movement of his troops," Mr. Reese said. "And with several thousand men, counting all the garrisons in the string of forts he's building, he would need those roads for the transportation of supplies, if for nothing else. I think it very sensible and far-sighted of him."

He turned to Daniel, who had been sitting quietly on the

18

floor, almost behind him. "Have you heard about those pack-horse brigades that haul the supplies from Fort Washington to Fort Greeneville and beyond?" Daniel was startled, for it almost seemed as if the stranger were addressing him alone.

"I—I've heard of 'em," he stammered quickly, for apparently Mr. Reese expected him to make a reply. "But I don't know much about 'em."

"Some of them are organized by the army, or the Legion as it is now called. There are detachments of infantry or dragoons to guard them on the march. Captain Benham is Pack-horse Master-General, and I have some little acquaintance with him. I am better known, however, to one of his subordinate captains —Mr. Sutherland."

"From what I hear," Mr. Worder said, "it's dangerous work. Always plenty of Indians lyin' about, waitin' in ambush to git hold of the meat and flour and ammunition they carry—not to mention the hosses."

Mr. Reese said smoothly, "But many of the brigades have military escort; most of them, I imagine."

Mrs. Worder stirred a little. "Time you children were asleep," she said not unkindly, for she knew how much a visit from a stranger like this meant to them in their lonely lives.

Mr. Reese rose at the very moment the young folk scrambled to their feet. "Time I was bedded down, too," he said with a laugh, "if I'm to get an early start tomorrow." He clapped young Daniel across the shoulder. "Want to come with me and join one of those pack-horse brigades we were talking about?"

Daniel was startled. "Why—I wouldn't know—" he began.

"You'd learn. It would be fine work for a lad like you. You

say you lost your pa to the Indians a while back. Here would be your chance to make some money and pay back the varmints at the same time."

Daniel looked quickly about him, searching the faces of the Worder family for some clue to the answer he must make. Neither Mr. nor Mrs. Worder's features told him anything— their expressions were almost masklike. The girls were open-mouthed. Luke looked excited; Jeptha and Abel stared at him stonily, Abel's mouth turned down in a half-sneer.

There was nothing to learn from their faces except that they would probably be glad to have him gone. He knew he had never been too welcome, but on the frontier one took in a neighbor's waif almost as a matter of course, and the Worders had done their duty, albeit with poor grace. They had fed him, as best they could, for three years now. Had he the right to stay on? Was the work that he could do repayment enough?

Mr. Reese clapped him again on the shoulder, and gave him a little push. "No need to answer now. Sleep on it, why don't you? Tell me in the morning what you decide."

Daniel stumbled up the ladder after the other boys as if he were climbing it in his sleep. Yet, when he had stretched out on his cornhusk pallet, he found himself wide awake. Long after the boys had begun to snore he stared into the darkness, shivering. Go farther into the wilderness, where bands of Indians lay in wait to massacre the unwary? Not he! And yet . . . perhaps he ought to.

Once he rose, and went toward the ladder, to tell Mr. Reese that the whole decision was too difficult for him. There was still enough light for him to make out the forms of Mr. Reese and his foster father standing by the stranger's quilt, spread before the hearth. He held his breath for a moment, and in that short space of time heard Mr. Worder say, "No, no, I'd really be glad if the young-un left. There's sometimes not enough food for so many hungry mouths. We've seven of our own, and another one comin', if all goes well. You can see how crowded we are here."

Daniel stole back to his bed and buried his face in his arms. He thought suddenly, This is the last night I'll be sleeping here. Where will I be tomorrow night? And all the tomorrows after that?

Two tears crept slowly from behind his tightly closed lids, and he brushed them away fiercely. From now on he would have to be on his own, like a man. . . . Only he wasn't a man yet.

CHAPTER TWO

Daniel hardly slept that night. Long before the first gray light appeared, he was up. He went silently down the ladder, his bare feet making no sound, and stepped over the sleeping forms on the cabin floor. Outside there was a faint chill in the air. This was the hour, he thought suddenly, when Indians often struck—the hour when sleep was sweetest, and there was no dream of danger. Silencing the dog with a reassuring hand, he closed the door behind him.

He stood for a moment, scanning the dark blur of the woods with an anxious eye, then moved beyond the lean-to where Mr. Reese's horse was tethered, until he came to the corncrib. It was nearly empty at this time of the year, and Daniel knew there would be lean weeks ahead until the new crop could be harvested. At the far end of the crib, he stooped and began to dig in the earth with his hands. When he touched something hard he gave a little grunt of satisfaction. The object was small and round, and he rubbed it against his deerskin leggings to remove the dirt. Then, thrusting it into the front of his shirt, he went back to the cabin.

There were signs of life by this time. Mrs. Worder was up and stirring, and Mr. Worder could be heard calling to the boys. Daniel tried to slip into the cabin unnoticed, but the sky was lighter now, even though the cabin was still dark, and when he opened the door enough of the dawn light came in with him to give him away.

"Why, Dan'l, you up a'ready?" Mrs. Worder said. "Best fetch me a couple logs, if we're goin' to have anything for breakfast."

He went out again, hurrying on his errand, for he did not want to miss Mr. Reese's departure. When he brought in the logs, Mr. Worder told him to saddle the horse for their visitor. The other boys came tumbling down from the loft. Mr. Reese sat up and stretched. Daniel did not move. He felt he must speak now or never.

"What's the matter, lad? Didn't you hear me tell you—" Mr. Worder began, a hint of anger in his voice.

"Yes, I know. I'll saddle up in a minute," Daniel said. His breath came short. "But afore I do, I wanted to ask—I wanted to say," he gulped, "that I'm goin' with Mr. Reese. I'd like to— to join one of the pack-horse brigades." His tongue almost refused the lie, but he managed to say it.

Mrs. Worder whirled around from the fireplace, and the children gawked at him. "You?" Abel cried, and his laugh was a hoot of derision. "You, that won't even go into the woods for fear you'll be scalped? What would *you* do, walkin' the trails with supplies the Indians would give their eyeteeth for?"

Daniel did not answer him. He looked at Mr. Worder instead. "I'd like to go." It was easier to say it the second time.

"Good lad!" Mr. Reese's hearty voice was like a steadying hand. "I'll be glad to have your company, for I gather I'll not

23

be able to make much speed on this section of the road. And I'll put in a word for you with my friend, Mr. Sutherland."

"Would you, sir?" Daniel tried to make his voice sound eager.

Mr. Worder shook his head. It was not a motion of denial, but of wonderment. "I'd never have thought such would be to your likin'," he said at last. "But if you want to go, why, there's nought to stop you."

Mrs. Worder said hastily, "He'll not be needin' his extra shirt. Luke could be wearin' that."

Daniel owned nothing but what he was wearing and that extra shirt, and Mrs. Worder had made that. Pride made him say, "Luke can have it." This was only another proof that he was not welcome in this household, that they would be glad to have him gone.

Later, when Daniel and Mr. Reese were moving down the road toward Columbia, he looked back on those last few minutes in the Worder household with disdain. Not only for the Worders, but for himself. If he had ever realized how little he was wanted, he would have left long since. A faint inner voice mocked at this, but he sternly silenced it.

"Do you have any money, lad?" Mr. Reese asked him, when they had been traveling a while.

"Money?" Daniel echoed. "No, sir." The very idea made him smile.

"But you didn't take anything with you," the man said, a slightly worried frown creasing his forehead. "Surely you must have had something left when your father was killed. I under-

stand your cabin was burned, but were there no tools or animals—nothing to salvage?"

Daniel's face was greenish under his tan as he remembered
that evil morning of discovery. "They stole our horse," he said,
as quietly as he could, "and they kilt the pigs, or druv them
off. The cow was burned so bad she died later. And Mr. Worder
kept whatever tools he could find—there weren't many es-
caped the fire—to pay for my board. I guess they didn't anywheres near do it, though. I've been with them almost three
years."

"Then you have nothing? Nothing at all?"

Daniel felt inside his shirt, where the round hard object
he had dug up that morning lay snugly. "I have a button," he
said slowly. "It was Pa's. They had ripped off the others, but
this one was still there." He glanced up shyly at Mr. Reese. "I
buried it so's the Worders wouldn't know I had it. But I
wanted something—" His voice would have broken if he hadn't
stopped then.

He marveled that he should tell this to a stranger, when
he had kept it secret all these many months from the Worders.
But he had felt an instinctive trust in this man. Surely, now,
his fortunes would take a turn for the better.

They talked, occasionally, on the road to Columbia, but
there was not always breath for conversation. When there was
a good stretch in the road, the horse wanted to move a little
faster, and Daniel had to run to keep up. Once or twice he rode
pillion for a distance, and one time Mr. Reese dismounted,
saying he wanted to stretch his legs a little, and insisting that
Daniel mount in his place.

25

They were in Columbia long before noon. It was almost four years since Daniel had been in a settlement of any kind. His father had landed at Columbia when they came down river to take up their land, but at the time Daniel had been so excited at thought of their new life in the woods, that he had scarcely noticed the life in the village. This time he was too excited at thought of what was coming when they reached Cincinnati, and so he was equally unobservant.

They enjoyed a brief rest with their meal, and then set off again. It was not far to Fort Washington, but the going was poor, and it was mid-afternoon by the time they reached it. Then Daniel really did gawk, for the sight of the trim soldiers, the stockade, and the five square blockhouses greatly impressed him.

Mr. Reese gave his name and was received shortly by an officer brave in buff and blue, his powdered hair smartly queued with a black ribbon. Daniel stared as if he could never see enough. He did not mind it when Mr. Reese asked him to wait while he went inside to speak with his friend. He squatted in the dust, holding the reins of Mr. Reese's horse, glad to rest for a while and eager to see as much of this strange place as possible. To think that yesterday, at this time, he'd not had the faintest idea of the new life that lay ahead of him!

When Mr. Reese came out, still accompanied by the handsome officer, Daniel saw at once that his new friend was troubled. He called the boy over to him and said, "Dan'l, I hope I have not done you a disservice. I thought that surely there would be a place for a bright lad like you with one of the packhorse brigades that the Legion sends out from here, but I am

FEAR IN THE FOREST

told that they are entirely composed of men enlisted for the purpose."

Daniel looked so puzzled that Mr. Reese had to smile a little. "I said 'men,' Dan'l, and you are not yet a man, though I doubt not you could give as good account of yourself as any man when it comes to work."

"Then there's nothing for me here?" Daniel said quietly, but his heart sank down to his dusty toes. Where would he turn now? How would he live? He was quite sure that he would not go back to the Worders, no matter how difficult things became.

"No, and I am sorry. But this gentleman tells me that there are civilian pack-horse trains in the employ of various contractors. There might be an opening for you with one of those. In fact, he has been kind enough to give me the names of several of the leaders, and some indication of where they may be found."

"I'd not want to take more of your time, Mr. Reese," Daniel said slowly. "If you'd give me the names, I'd hunt them up myself."

"That's a good lad," the officer said. But his voice was casual, and he turned to Mr. Reese with relief. "Then you and I could go into this matter further. Since Mr. Sutherland is not here, I hope you will be my guest. I should be honored to introduce you to the mess."

Mr. Reese smiled. "Not a bad idea. But, mind you, my lad," he turned an earnest gaze upon Daniel, "mind you, if you cannot find any of these men, or if you are unable to find employment with them, come back here, and I shall undertake further inquiries on your behalf."

"I believe there are only two of them in town at the moment," the officer said. "Ask for Josiah Gregg at the White Horse, or for Robert MacLeish at the Green Tree tavern."

They turned back and Daniel, feeling suddenly very alone in the world, tied the horse to a hitching post and went slowly out through the gate of the fort. The sentry was kind enough to tell him how to reach the two taverns the officer had mentioned, and Daniel scuffed through the dust reluctantly, hardly glancing at the town ahead, or at the Ohio River on his left.

"Josiah Gregg?" the tavern-keeper said. "Just left here a couple minutes past, nor do I know where he went, so don't ask me. He's a busy man and it might have been any one of twenty places." His eyes took in Daniel's ragged appearance, and hardened. "Was there anything else you wanted—some food or drink, perhaps?" But his voice showed all too plainly that he doubted if Daniel would have the money to pay for either.

"Will he be coming back here?" Daniel asked, not answering the man's question. "Because if he will, I'll wait for him. . . . Outside," he added quickly, seeing the man's frown.

"He'll be back. He owes me for feeding his men, and he's honest so he'll pay me." The tavern-keeper turned away to raise a heavy stewpot hanging on the crane, and Daniel slipped outside.

He squatted down with his back against the wall of the tavern to wait. He was tired and, although he knew he should be hunting for Mr. MacLeish since Josiah Gregg was not to be found, it felt good to sit here for a while and watch the passing stream of people. After life on the Worder farm, it seemed to

The sentry told him how to reach the taverns.

him that at least half the people in the United States must be here on Cincinnati's water front.

A tall boy, older than he, came to sit beside Daniel after a few minutes. They sat in silence, each one too shy to start talking, until the boy said, "You live here? I don't recollect seein' you."

Daniel said, "I come from north of Columbia. I been livin' on a farm there."

"You down here for supplies?"

"No."

"Your pa sold the place?"

"No. Pa got kilt by the Indians three years ago."

"You ain't been livin' there all alone with your ma!" the other boy cried, startled out of his casual manner.

"Ma's dead. Died when I was eight. We lived in Pennsylvania then."

There was a silence until it dawned on Daniel that the other boy wanted to know with whom he *had* been living, if not with his ma. For it was obvious that he could not have been living by himself. He added, "I been livin' with the Worders. They had the next farm. Do you know them?"

"No."

For a while the conversation came to a standstill. Then, suddenly, Daniel realized that if this boy was a native of Cincinnati he might know something about the man he was searching for. "Do you know Josiah Gregg?" he asked.

The boy turned his head quickly, to look at him with a glance that was actually challenging. "You jokin'?" he said at last. "He's my pa."

30

Daniel's smile was so relieved that the other boy relaxed at once.

"What do you know?" Daniel cried. "I been lookin' for him. I want to ask him if he'll hire me. Mr. Reese and the officer at the fort said he might. My name's Dan'l. I'm right strong, and I can handle animals pretty well. Though the Worders didn't have a horse—only an ox. Jonas was his name, and he was pretty poky, I can tell you. But I know I could—"

"Hey! Wait a minute!" the other boy laughed. "Pa's the one does the hirin'. I only work for him."

Daniel felt a little reassured. This boy might be fourteen, which was two years older than he was, but the very fact that Mr. Gregg had a lad working for him was a good sign. If he had one, maybe he'd take another one. The other boy was speaking again. "My name's Amos," he said. Then, with a searching look, "It's hard work, you know. And it can be right dangerous. You sure that's what you want to do?"

Daniel lowered his eyes so that Amos would not see the fear in them. "Yes, it is," he said stoutly.

"Well, I'll put in a good word for you, but that don't mean much." Amos started to laugh, but stopped abruptly and got to his feet. "Here's Pa now," he said, as a tall man approached them. "Pa, this is Dan'l. He ain't got no folks, and he wants to work for you. You got a place for him?"

"I got a place, but I don't know if it's for him," the big man answered slowly. He stood before Daniel, towering over him and over his son—a good six feet of bone and muscle. His beard was thick and had a reddish tinge, and his eyes were a piercing blue. He hooked his thumbs in his belt and stared at Daniel. Daniel tried to stand straight and look strong and competent.

"You ain't got no folks, Amos says." It was half a question.

"His ma died in Pennsylvania, and his pa was kilt by the Indians," Amos supplied.

"Let the lad do his own talkin', Amos," Josiah Gregg said in a mild voice.

"That's right," Daniel said at once. "I been livin' with the Worders on their farm. It's north of Columbia a ways. They had the farm nearest Pa's."

"And why do you want to leave?"

Daniel looked up, and found his eyes held by the bright blue ones of Josiah. He said truthfully, "They have seven children, and there wasn't always enough to go around. I thought I better start makin' my own way."

"And how old are you?"

"Twelve." It didn't sound like much when he said it. He hoped it sounded like much more to Mr. Gregg.

"Twelve. . . . Come to think of it, I believe I could use a boy of about twelve. Of course you're not a man yet, so you'd not git a man's pay. I hope you don't mind hard work!"

There was a twinkle in the man's eyes, Daniel was sure. He said, with a gasp, "Not I, sir!"

"Then I'll put Amos in charge of you. Amos, see that he has what he needs—he ought to have a pair of moccasins—and feed him up a little, then come down to the camp. There's plenty still to do, and I want to get started tomorrow. Now, make tracks."

He strode off, and Daniel, his eyes shining, stared after him.

For the moment he had forgotten the dangers that might lay ahead, and only knew that here was a man he could trust, a man he'd be glad to work for.

"Come on!" Amos said, starting off in the opposite direction. "When Pa says 'Make tracks,' we make tracks. There's a place down here where we can git you a pair of moccasins."

CHAPTER THREE

The road was easy enough to follow. Soldiers had widened it, and their marching feet and the passage of many horses and supply wagons had packed it down in ruts in the dry places and had hopelessly mired it in the wet ones. Daniel strode along happily in his new moccasins.

He kept his eyes fastened upon Amos ahead of him. Amos was big for fourteen. His frame showed promise of being as large, if not larger, than his father's. His ready grin, whenever he looked back, warmed Daniel's heart in a fashion he had never known. But then, he had never had a friend before.

"Won't git to Fort Hamilton afore nightfall," growled Timothy, the man who drove the string of horses behind Daniel. He had a portly figure and a fat, petulant face beneath an untidy stubble of beard. He was inclined to lag, and Henry, the man who drove the string behind him, sometimes had to call out to him to press on a little faster.

"How far is it to Fort Hamilton?" Daniel asked Amos.

"About twenty-five mile," Amos answered. "Usually we make it from fort to fort in a day's travel, but too many things went wrong this morning, and we didn't get started as early as we should've."

Daniel's heart shook, but he managed to keep his voice steady as he asked, "Then we'll—have to camp out tonight?"

"I reckon. But I wouldn't wonder Pa has it in mind to stop at our farm."

"Do you live on this road?"

"Not far off'n it. Not far from Fort Hamilton, neither. Pretty close to where Dunlap's Station was. You ever hear of Dunlap's Station?"

"Yes. . . . I've heard of it." He got the words out, but they almost stuck in his throat. He could remember the winter night when a trader—one of the few visitors he and his father had ever had—sat comfortably before their cabin fire and told about it.

"Only twenty-eight men in the station," the trader had said, "and pretty near five hunnerd Indians! A regular siege it was. But they stuck it out, and chased the critters away afore help came from Fort Washington. I heard tell the women melted down all their pewter plates to make bullets afore the men scared off the varmints."

His father had said, "Who led them? It's not like Indians to attack in such force. They must have had a leader."

The trader was thoughtful. "Folks say it was Girty, and I wouldn't be surprised but it was, though the white man—for it was a white man led 'em—stood too far away to be recognized. Worse'n an Indian he was. They tortured one poor fellow they captured, though he begged his friends to surrender so's he'd be saved, and they done it right in full view of the station. They say Girty put 'em up to it."

Daniel remembered that he had ventured in a small voice, "But why didn't they surrender to save the man?"

The trader had laughed a little, and his father had smiled

35

at him. "And what would have happened to the twenty-eight men in the fort when they surrendered?" the trader asked. He answered his own question. "They'd have been tortured, too, every last one of 'em, or carried off as prisoners to run the gantlet. I'm glad to say they had more sense than to listen to poor Abner Hunt, though it must have been hard to close their ears to his screams."

Daniel shivered now as he had shivered that night. Cruelty like that was something impossible to understand. Perhaps he had had a sort of premonition, too. It was that very same year —but in the fall season—that his father had been killed, and he had become homeless.

Suddenly he shouted, and the column of horses came slowly to a halt. Amos turned back to him as Ben, the second in command, ran up from the rear. "What's up?"

But they did not need an answer, for Daniel stood alongside one of the pack-horses, his shoulder braced against the pack which threatened to slip off to one side in a moment.

Ben grunted in annoyance, and while he and Amos and Daniel worked to right the load and tighten the hitch, he said, "Who loaded this pony? Timothy, wasn't it?"

Timothy, a little to the rear, heard him. "Not me! Simon, I'll bet. He don't know his hand from his foot most of the time."

But Daniel distinctly remembered that it *was* Timothy who had loaded this particular horse. He remembered because the horse had a notched right ear, and Timothy's right ear was lacking most of the lobe. He had even commented on it to Amos, and Amos had said, with a laugh, "Lost it in a fight, most likely.

Timothy, I mean, not the hoss! Some of the fights on the water front at Cincinnati can be mighty rough."

Daniel wondered if he should speak out. It was not right that slow, good-natured Simon should take the blame for Timothy's careless work, but he was still so new to the troop, and still so much on trial that he didn't dare. But he tucked away the knowledge that Timothy was not only careless, but would lie about it.

When they were on the move again, he resumed his shouted conversation with Amos. "You folks got a big farm?"

"Too big, when I'm home and have chores to do!" Amos called back. "But Pa isn't workin' only a piece of it yet. The family can take care of what's growin', and the stock, too, while he and I go out to earn a little. We want to buy some more cows, and we need more sheep—the wolves got most of 'em last winter—and things like salt and gunpowder and lead are so high we figured we'd better get us some real buyin' money."

There was silence between them for a while, as Daniel digested this information. The Greggs must have several cows, and if the wolves had killed off a lot of their sheep in the winter they must have had a number of those, too. Mr. Gregg, Daniel decided, was pretty near a rich man to have so much livestock. He must have a big family, too, if they could take care of his farm while he captained a pack-horse train with his son.

It was late afternoon when the troop made a slight detour to the right of the road. A narrow rutted path led through deep woods to a clearing in the center of which stood a four-square cabin with well-chinked walls and a stout chimney. A young child, playing in front of the house, saw them first, and shouted with glee. The dogs came running, and at once the rest of the family appeared in the doorway: two half-grown boys, as alike as two peas, a tawny-haired girl, and a plump, motherly-looking woman.

They all ran forward and threw themselves upon Mr. Gregg, laughing and hugging, and all talking at once. Amos, watching them with a smile, said to Daniel proudly, "That's my folks! Just my luck to git here in time for chores, wasn't it?" But Daniel could see he was happy to be home.

The men made camp, as they would have if they were settling down for the night beside one of Anthony Wayne's string of forts instead of in the house-clearing of a farm. Josiah, after that first warm greeting from his family, was all business. He and Ben were everywhere at once, instructing, helping, staking out the area where the animals were to be grazed, where the packs were to lie, where the men were to bivouac, and where the campfire was to be built.

"There'll be no need to cook tonight," Simon said happily. "We been here afore, and Mrs. Gregg sets a mighty fine table. I hope she's been expectin' us."

As it turned out, the visit was a surprise, and Mrs. Gregg and Polly, the tawny-haired girl, who looked to be just about Daniel's age, began cooking and baking at once. Amos turned the work of unloading his horses over to Simon so that he could help the twins, Ethan and Judah, with the chores, and Daniel ran to help, too, as soon as he could.

The cows had already been rounded up, and Polly had milked some of them, but now there was not time for her to

Mrs. Gregg and Polly began cooking at once.

finish the job. "I reckon we'll have to do it," Amos said mournfully as he and Daniel led the animals behind the cabin where they wouldn't be seen. Milking was woman's work, and boys and men did not want to be seen doing it when it was necessary to take over the chore.

"You hold her and I'll milk her," Amos said, approaching the first cow warily, a stool in one hand and a wooden bucket in the other. "She likes to wait till you're most done, and then kick the bucket over. Got a mean temper, this one has." So Daniel held the cow while Amos milked, and then Amos held the next cow while Daniel milked. He was awkward at it, for there had been enough girls in the Worder household so that he had seldom done it before.

With the milking over, they raced to the woodpile to bring in logs. And after that there was fodder to fetch for the horses, and water from the spring. By the time they had finished, Mrs. Gregg and Polly had supper ready, and it was beginning to get dark.

They all ate out-of-doors, sitting in a circle around the men's campfire. The food was simple but tasty, and Daniel decided that Mrs. Gregg was a handy cook. The johnnycake was hot and had a delicious flavor, and the mush-and-milk was sweetened with maple sugar. There was boiled salt pork and sweet potatoes and garden greens. Altogether, it was no supper but a feast!

The men ate greedily, yet Timothy outdid them all. No wonder he's so fat, Daniel thought, watching him stuff food into his wide mouth. But there was enough to go around, and some left over.

Ethan and Judah tumbled over each other like two half-grown puppies, and little Sabrina, the baby, crept over the men's legs and dipped her fingers into every plate. Polly caught her up several times and returned her to her mother, but Mrs. Gregg was too busy to hold her, and in no time at all Sabrina was back again, crawling from one to another.

Finally Josiah took her on his lap, where she curled up and promptly fell asleep. The dogs circled hungrily, asking for scraps, and as the men's hunger was satisfied and the fire began to die down, talk grew louder and more continuous.

Daniel was fascinated by the different faces. The strong planes of Josiah Gregg's face were emphasized by the firelight, so that it had the look of being carved from some glowing metal. Mrs. Gregg, on the other hand, seemed years younger now and prettier, with the rosy appearance of a girl. Henry, who sat on Josiah's right hand, had a dreamy air and his eyes showed deeply sunk in their sockets. Simon's usually dull face took on new life and the flicker of light seemed to create expressions which came and vanished within split seconds.

Timothy's jowls threw dark shadows when the flames shot high, and his small eyes were half-closed against the light, making him look more like a pig than ever. Ben, short and stocky and tough, might have been a young lad, with all the strong lines of his face softened in the glare.

Daniel turned to look at Polly who sat on his right, and found her watching him. "What were you thinkin' about?" she asked suddenly, as direct in approach as any boy.

It surprised him, for she had not said two words to him as yet. Of course, she had been busy helping her mother prepare the quantities of food the men had consumed. But there had been time enough for laughing remarks to her brothers, to her father and to Ben and Henry, both of whom she seemed to know well. With Daniel she had been tongue-tied, yet he had sensed that it was not because of shyness, but only because she did not yet know him.

He realized that he had not answered her, and smiled and shook his head. "I don't know what I was thinkin', exactly," he confessed. "It was more like watchin' and feelin'. I was watchin' people's faces, and how they looked in the firelight. Some it changes, and others it—it just makes them look more like what they are."

She seemed to understand what he meant, and nodded agreement. "Mebbe people show what they are really like around a fire because they know they're partly in the dark, and they don't expect they show as much as they do."

He was pleased. That was just what he had had in mind, but it had been difficult to express. "You said you were feelin', too," she prodded him. "Feelin' what?"

This was even harder to say, but he made a try at it. "Feelin' what it was like here—at your place. It's like it was when we lived in Pennsylvania. When my ma was still livin', and we were all together."

"Sort of a family feelin'?" she asked, after a moment's pondering.

"That's it—a family feelin'. And it's funny," he added, "that I never had it when I lived with the Worders. They were a family—a big one—but it wasn't the same. Leastways, not for me it wasn't."

He had not realized how silent the others had become as he talked, and it was only with the last words he spoke that he sensed how loud they sounded. He glanced about, embarrassed, but he found the Greggs all smiling at him, and Ben and Henry, too. Even dull Simon's face wore a sheepish grin. Timothy was still eating, and did not look up.

"Tell Ma your story, son," Josiah Gregg commanded. And when Daniel did not speak at once, he said to his wife, "The lad was born in Pennsylvania, and when his ma died there, his pa sold out and came west to take up land along the Little Miami. Now, you go on from there, Dan'l."

Daniel swallowed hard. Could he make these people understand what had hung over him like a cloud since that terrible October day? He said slowly, "We had neighbors in Pennsylvania, but where Pa settled, above Columbia, we were as good as alone. The Worders lived next us, but they were a couple miles farther down the river and off to the west. Pa cleared a place for our cabin, and put it up all by himself. I helped him some, but I was only eight then.

"We had a horse and a cow, and Pa had bought some pigs so's we'd have a start, and wouldn't have to eat game all the time. He worked hard, but of course he couldn't clear much, bein' all alone that way. The woods were—awful close. . . ."

He swallowed again. "We had a good harvest that first year, and Pa said he'd got a prime piece of land. He was diggin' a pit for some of the root vegetables we'd raised, and he sent me out to the woods to do some berryin'. He'd traded a pig for some sweetenin' and said he'd a mind to have somethin' besides meat when winter came. I was out there—in the woods—when I heard them."

The silence was broken by Timothy. "Heard who?" he asked, his mouth full.

"The Indians. I heard them yellin' first, and then I heard shots. I hadn't anythin' but the wooden bucket in my hand. I ran back towards the cabin, but by the time I got there it was burnin' fierce. I couldn't see Pa nowheres, and I figured he'd mebbe got away. The Indians were quiet then, but I didn't know whether they were waitin' in the woods for me to come out, or whether they were really gone. So I crept back a ways, and waited. I waited till it got dark, and I waited all night. It was—cold. And I was scairt."

He stopped then. This was the hardest part to tell, or almost the hardest part. But Mrs. Gregg's face was alive with sympathy, and he could feel the eyes of Polly and Amos full upon him, waiting for the rest of the story. His fingers reached up to touch the pewter button hidden inside his shirt.

"I found Pa in the half-dug pit," he said at last. "He'd been shot, and scalped, and pretty well hacked up. They'd ripped most of his clothes off. They'd kilt the cow and some of the pigs. They'd druv off the others, and the horse, too. They took everything they could lay their hands to."

"You poor lad! What did you do then?" Mrs. Gregg asked.

Polly seized his hand and gave it a quick squeeze, as if to say by touch what she could not put into words.

"I ran to the Worders. Mr. Worder wouldn't go back with me, but he sent around to some other folks that didn't live too far away, and the men went back together and buried Pa. After

44

that, I hadn't nowheres to go, so I lived with the Worders. But they had six children—it's seven now—and there wasn't rightly room for me, I guess."

Polly said fiercely, "I should think there'd always be room for somebody like you!"

And Amos said, "Sure. It's not as if you weren't willin' to do your share. You can come and live with us, Dan'l, any time you want."

It was said lightly, as if to ease the feeling of tragedy which Daniel's story had brought to the circle around the fire. Daniel didn't think Amos really meant it, but it cheered him, just the same, and make him feel wanted, the way Polly's indignant speech had. He hugged their words to him and found them comforting.

But there was still the hardest part to come. He took a deep breath. "I was afeared the day Pa was kilt," he said bravely, "and I've been afeared ever since. I'm afeared of the woods. Sometimes I think I hear an Indian behind every tree. And there's an awful lot of trees!" His laugh was a little hollow.

"I should think you would be scairt," Mrs. Gregg said simply. "Shows you've got feelin's."

Polly was thoughtful. "I reckon most folks that live like we do get scairt plenty of times. Because there's plenty to be scairt of! But there's lots of other things, too—work, and growin' crops where there was only woods before, and makin' a home, and huntin', and—and all kinds of things. You can't enjoy any of 'em if you let yourself be scairt *all* the time. So you have to keep the scairt feelin' for when there's something to be scairt of!" She turned eagerly to Daniel. "Do you see what I mean?"

"Yes," he said slowly. "I hadn't thought of it like that. I *would* like workin' the land, and I *would* like huntin', if it wasn't for the Indians. So mebbe I'd just better stop bein' afeared." He smiled at her, a new resolve forming from this moment of understanding.

CHAPTER FOUR

The pack-horse train was on its way early the next morning. Josiah Gregg said a fond farewell to his wife, and Amos turned to wave to the family as long as he could see them. Then the forest swallowed them up again. It was not long before there were glimpses of the Miami River.

They came to an immense meadow, or prairie, covered with high grass, and Daniel was surprised to see men scything the grass. They wore the uniform of the Legion.

"Cuttin' hay for the hosses at the fort," Amos said. "Now we'll be seein' the fort soon. It's only a mile from here."

They passed a wagon train on its way south. The wagons creaked and groaned, lurching over the rough road, and the slow oxen turned patient eyes toward the group. There was a convoy of soldiers who called out and exchanged greetings with them.

Fort Hamilton lay lengthwise along the river, its double row of stout pickets and four blockhouses offering a feeling of protection against the wilderness and the dangers of Indian attack. Josiah stopped briefly to go within the stockade and speak to the officer in charge of the commissary, but Daniel knew, from the talk he had heard at Cincinnati, that they had nothing for Fort Hamilton this trip. All their supplies were for Fort Greeneville.

He cast many backward glances as they moved northward, crossing the river well above the fort and continuing upon General Wayne's military road along Seven Mile Creek. Here the country was prairielike again, with only low hills on their right at some distance. On the other side of the creek the hills rose steeply.

Amos called back to Daniel, "See all those wild-pea vines? Pa says we could pasture a whole herd of cattle here without turnin' a hand! He says if he'd known about this afore he settled on our farm, he'd have chosen this place. Good sandy soil, too! It'll grow most anything, I reckon. I tell him I'm goin' to take up land here when I'm grown. By that time Gen'l Wayne should ha' knocked some sense into the Indians."

"Harmar couldn't do it," growled Timothy behind them. "Nor St. Clair, neither. Worst defeat we ever had was when St. Clair tried it. Why could Anthony Wayne do it when they couldn't? Tell me that!"

"Because he's a better gen'l."

"Can't tell *me* he's a good gen'l! Runs his men ragged, he does. Marches 'em all over creation, makes 'em swim rivers or drown—and he don't care, neither, if they *do* drown—has 'em tearin' all over the parade ground, trailin' their guns and yellin' like a bunch o' Indians themselves. What kind of army does he think he's got? Nothin' that'll stand up agin the Indians when the time comes, I can tell you!"

"The only way to fight Indians is to do what they do, only better!" Amos cried indignantly. "That's why Gen'l Wayne is teachin' his men to be good marksmen and woods fighters. And they won't be scairt of Indian whoops and hollers, neither, because they'll be makin' so much noise themselves they won't hear the Indians. It's just common sense, that's all."

"Well, the men don't think so. I used to hear many of them talkin' about him in the taverns at Cincinnati, whenever they could git away from Hobson's Choice. 'Old Toney,' they called him, or even 'Toney Lumpkin,' which is worse. Can't tell *me* a gen'l what's called 'Toney Lumpkin' by his very own men can be any good."

Amos snorted, but had no chance to carry the argument further. One of his horses broke loose at that point and had to be chased and cornered and brought back to the string he and Daniel were in charge of. Once the runaway was tied into place again, Amos would have said more, but by that time the boys were farther back in the line, too far from Timothy.

When they stopped that noon to rest and eat, they had covered quite some distance. "We'll make it to Fort St. Clair today, easy," Ben said with satisfaction. "The forts were laid out so's they'd be just a day's journey apart for the supply trains. Washington, Hamilton, St. Clair, and Jefferson. Greeneville's only a few miles farther."

"A good thing they were laid out like that, too," Josiah said, "for if there's one thing an Indian wants to lay his hands on— always takin' into account that scalps come first with 'em—it's a hoss. And a hoss that's carryin' flour or meat, or arms or ammunition is as good as treasure to 'em."

Daniel shrank inwardly. The idea was never too far from his mind that there might be Indians lurking nearby, watching and waiting for the chance to ambush and kill. Now it was brought into startling focus by learning that their favorite

49

quarry was a pack-horse train. His head jerked involuntarily to one side, and he stared into the woods along the road. But pride made him jerk it back again almost as quickly.

"Pa's made this trip many a time," Amos said the moment Josiah had finished speaking. Daniel knew his friend had seen his movement of fear, and flushed with shame. "But he's never laid eyes on any Indians except once or twice when a party of 'em come to one of the forts. And they were peace parties—or said they were."

Simon said suddenly, "My folks was from Kentucky. They lost so many neighbors, kilt by the Indians, that they crossed the Ohio."

"Whatever for?" Henry asked. "Ohio was settled later, so there was more risk."

"I dunno." Simon smiled his foolish smile, and tucked his chin in a little. "I reckon they didn't want to go back to Virginny, and they didn't want to go west account of the Spanish, so they went north."

Daniel thought suddenly, Everyone who has come to the Northwest Territory has come for a reason. His own father had come because of a restlessness after he had lost his wife. Simon's people had headed right into the Indian country because their neighbors had been killed off by the Indians! The Worders had come because Mr. Worder was land-hungry and could not afford to buy a big enough farm in the east. The Greggs—

"Why did your folks come out here to settle?" he asked Amos.

"I reckon we're the movin' kind," Amos answered with a chuckle. "Pa's folks a couple generations back went from New

50

England to Jersey. And Pa's father went from Jersey to Pennsylvania. Pa felt it was gettin' too settled there, I think, so he packed us up and moved on here. He says he don't like crowdin', but I think it's just an itch to keep movin', myself."

Daniel frowned a little. His own instinct was to find a safe place and stay there. He said, "But there's all that work each time. Findin' a good place, with water and good soil, and clearin' the land, and buildin' a house and sheds and all. Seems to me, he'd ha' been a rich man if he and his folks had stayed put in the first place."

Amos laughed outright. "Not if you'd heard my grandfather tell the stories *his* pa told about the soil in New England! Too barren to raise anythin' but rocks, he used to say. And even those wasn't respectable big rocks, but just middle-sized ones that broke his plow if he left 'em lie, and broke his back if he tried to carry 'em off'n the field."

Daniel laughed too, a little. But he meant what he had said. The idea of perpetually going on to new, and supposedly better, lands left him uninterested. Maybe he had no sense of adventure, he thought, but at any rate he could see how impractical it was to put so much labor into creating a new farm, only to leave it in a generation and start all over again somewhere else.

The air was close when they got to Fort St. Clair, and Daniel would have liked to rest in the shade of a massive oak near the pickets. They had made good time that day despite the heat and the extra distance, for the men had pushed their horses toward the end, wanting to make their encampment and get things settled for the night while it was still light.

There was no chance to rest; there was too much to do.

When they unloaded the animals, Josiah saw that several of them had their backs and sides rubbed sore from the loads they carried. Without hesitation, he rounded on Timothy with an angry bellow.

"You! You're no more a pack-horse man than a ring-tailed rabbit! I thought so when you was hired, and now I'm sure of it. Why, Dan'l here is a sight handier with animals than you are! These are your critters, and don't try to crawfish out'n it by saying they ain't. If you'd taken a little more pains in the loadin' of 'em, this wouldn't have happened. Now, get out of my sight afore I do you a harm."

Timothy shambled away, his little pig-eyes narrowed, his neck red and swelling with repressed fury. The glance he darted at Daniel was not reassuring, and the boy thought, Now he's a-goin' to have it in for me because of what Mr. Gregg said.

Daniel and Amos helped with the treating of the sore horses. They cleaned the raw places with water from one of the clear springs, while a knot of soldiers stood and watched them. Then they rubbed on a heavy salve that Josiah fetched from his personal bundle.

"I doubt they'll be fit for the next trip up," Amos sighed. "Though we travel light on the way back, sores like these won't be well in three-four days' time."

"It's a shame to treat beasts so." Daniel was indignant.

"This is bad enough," Josiah said with a shake of his head, "but you should see some of the animals I've seen. There's been such a call for supplies for the Legion that some men have been loadin' kegs of powder and flour and lumber on the poor critters without so much as a blanket to take the rubbin'. Those hosses are ruined for fair in one trip."

One of the soldiers spoke. "Wagon hosses, too," he said "Some of the wagon trains come through with the critters half dead. Just a few days ago, when Colonel Strong come through with a wagon train and a convoy of dragoons, they was pretty winded."

"Winded?" Josiah asked with an upward glance as he bent over one of the ponies.

"Aye. His spies got sight of a big force of Indians—two-three hunnerd of 'em—so the whole train come a-peltin' into the fort for safety. The more spies the colonel sent out, the more Indians they found. He sent off for orders afore he would go on again."

Daniel pressed hard upon the flank of the horse he was salving so that the trembling of his hand would not be seen. Indians! Here! And only a few days ago.

"Lose any men?" Josiah asked.

"Naw, not that time. But there's Indians all around. And, of course, the farther north you go, the more Indians."

Josiah straightened, and slapped the pony on the rump. "Tether these nearby, Ben," he said to his second-in-command. "Don't want them roamin' afield tonight." He wiped his hands on some dry grass. "We'll have to git in some fresh meat," he said. "Ma sent along enough food for this noon, and we'll still have some johnnycake left, but somebody ought to do a little huntin'." His gaze rested speculatively on Daniel, and Daniel tried to make himself as small as possible.

"I'll go," Simon volunteered.

"No, you went last time. It's best we take turns, I think.

Amos, it's your turn. Think you can find us something to eat?" his father asked with a twinkle.

"I'll take care of your hosses," Daniel said quickly to his friend.

"Oh, I won't go until we've made camp for the night. It's still early," Amos said. "I thought mebbe you'd like to go along with me."

Daniel knew what Amos was trying to do, and his heart lifted. If he went with Amos, he wouldn't be sent alone later. It would be easier to venture into the woods with another. He said, at once, "Sure. But I have no gun."

"Pa'll lend you one."

So that was settled. Henry agreed to hobble their horses, once they had unloaded, and Daniel set out, experiencing alternate shivers of fear and excitement. He would have liked hunting if he had not been so afraid of the Indians. He was a good shot, too.

He cast only one longing glance backward at the snug fort, thinking enviously of those who shared its shelter, but he had little time for regrets. Amos, walking through the woods like an Indian, toe first on rock and heel first on grass, was expecting him to be on the alert.

It was Amos who first saw the pheasants. He stopped abruptly and Daniel almost bumped into him. They had agreed before setting out that if they came upon more than one piece of game at a time, Amos was to take the one on the left, and Daniel the one on the right. Their guns spoke almost in unison, and the pheasants were theirs.

Amos caught them up and tucked them into the front of his

voluminous hunting shirt. "I could wish they came a mite larger," he chuckled. "About buffalo size would suit me fine."

"You'd never be able to carry them then," Daniel grinned. "I hope you ain't expectin' anything very big so near the fort—game must be pretty well shot up around a place like this."

"Oh, I don't know," Amos retorted with a toss of his head. "Like as not the men at the fort ain't allowed to go out huntin' —leastways not in small parties. So there ought to be plenty game left."

Leastways not in small parties. . . . Daniel knew why. It was too dangerous. There were too many Indians about. Yet here he was, with only Amos for company, in the deep woods that grew only a few hundred feet beyond the fort. All his old fear rushed back upon him, and he would have liked to turn tail and run.

Perhaps Amos sensed this. Perhaps he, too, was eager to finish the hunt. At any rate, not five minutes later, he suddenly reached out to tug at Daniel's sleeve. "Now, there's a likely place for a bear to hide," he said, scarcely bothering to keep his voice down or his footsteps soft as he strode ahead. He pointed to a huge sycamore tree, many feet in circumference, which was hollowed out at the base. The hole was as wide as a door, Daniel thought, and almost as high.

The words had no sooner left Amos' lips than a great black shape came lumbering out of the hole. Amos sped off to the left and climbed a tree with astonishing speed. Daniel, in his hurry to find a tree of his own to climb, dropped his gun.

Safe for a moment in the lower branches, he called to Amos, "He'll be comin' up after us! Bears can climb!"

"I know that, want-wit!" Amos retorted, aiming carefully. He pulled the trigger, and the shot sounded loud in Daniel's ears. He fully expected to see the bear fall in a heap, but the great creature only shook itself as if a bee had stung it, and made purposefully for Amos' tree.

Daniel shinnied down his own tree and darted forward to retrieve his gun. The bear did not seem to notice him at all. It advanced on Amos' tree with deliberation while Amos, far above him, worked frantically to reload. Daniel braced himself, drew a careful bead upon the bear, and fired.

This time the bear advanced another two steps, then suddenly, as if it had been pole-axed, dropped to the ground and lay perfectly still.

56

"D'you think it's playin' 'possum?" Amos called out. "Watch out it don't raise up and grab you!"

But Daniel knew with complete certainty that his shot had hit a vital spot. He went forward and boldly poked at the bear with his gun barrel. It did not stir.

"Wait till the others hear about this!" Amos, breathless from his quick descent from the tree, came racing over to where Daniel stood. "They'll never believe that we got one so close to the fort—and such a big one. That *you* got one," he amended quickly, "for it was you that shot him."

Daniel said, "But I couldn't have shot him if you hadn't held him till I got my gun. I was a fool to drop it in the first place."

The boys set about skinning the bear, or as much of it as they would be able to carry back to the camp. A quick glance upward told them that there might still be light enough for some of the others to come into the woods and retrieve the rest of the animal.

"Um-m, bear stew," Amos said, "and a good fat bear, too. Ma's partial to bear oil. I only wish I could save her some of this critter's fat." Suddenly he looked over at Daniel, his face puzzled. "You were mighty cool when this bear took after us," he commented. "'Cept for droppin' your gun, which could happen to anybody. And the way you went after him, without nothin' in your hands! Why, I thought you—" He broke off, and colored with embarrassment.

"I'm only afeared of Indians," Daniel said. Now that the bear had been killed, he remembered that he was alone in the slowly darkening woods, except for Amos. Amos, and who knew how many Indians. Indians were always lurking about Anthony Wayne's forts, people said. There might be one behind any of the distant trees. Or more than one. After all, there had been a number of shots to draw their attention.

He struggled bravely with his fear, and this time was sure that he kept it from showing on his face. That, at least, was achievement.

CHAPTER FIVE

That night Daniel found it hard to sleep. He turned from side to side, unable to find a comfortable position on the hard ground. For the first time since joining the pack-horse troop he thought with something like longing of his cornhusk pallet at the Worders' homestead.

The campfire had burned to embers when he saw Timothy rise from his place nearby. Instinctively, remembering the man's threatening glance, Daniel tensed in expectation of attack. But Timothy walked noiselessly around him, skirting the sleepers with the same care, and disappeared into the woods where the horses were hobbled.

Daniel half rose to go after him, but the thought of the dark woods held him back. Although Indians seldom attacked in the middle of the night, preferring the hush just before dawn, his mind peopled the forest with hundreds of Miamis and Shawnees.

And then he remembered the horses. Was Timothy the sort who would vent his spleen on helpless animals? Would he injure more of the pack-horses in some devious way? Without stopping to think further, Daniel rose to his feet with caution and slipped silently after the bulky figure ahead of him.

Once his eyes had adjusted to the gloom of the forest, he did not find it too difficult to follow Timothy who made no effort to be quiet when he was hidden from his comrades. But Daniel still held his breath and moved quickly from tree to tree.

The woods thinned suddenly to a natural glade and Daniel, his breath caught in a gasp, came to a halt. Ahead of him Timothy was walking forward confidently to greet another man. In the dimness and at this distance, Daniel could not tell whether it was a white man or an Indian, and at the thought that it might be the latter he began to tremble. There was a roaring in his ears as he fought his panic. Now he must be completely silent, he knew, for if it *was* an Indian, his life was surely forfeit. His hand sought the pewter button inside his shirt and touched it for comfort.

The two men talked together briefly and something passed between them, but Daniel could not see what it was. He was glad when the other man turned away at the conclusion of their talk and disappeared into the woods beyond. That gave Daniel the chance to edge around the tree which concealed him, so that Timothy would not see him. They returned to the campfire, Daniel always a good distance behind Timothy as before.

But now, when Timothy had once more lain down beside the others, Daniel faced a real problem. How could *he* return unnoticed? Not only by the others, but especially by Timothy. If Timothy were to suspect that Daniel had seen him at his rendezvous, and if that rendezvous was what Daniel thought it was, there was real trouble ahead.

Daniel paused at the edge of the forest. Had Timothy seen his empty place at the campfire? What could he do that would seem natural and unsuspicious? Suddenly he remembered that the injured horses were tethered nearby for the night, not roaming as freely as the others in the train. He headed toward them.

He made no effort to be quiet when he returned to the camp-fire. Josiah roused to a sitting position at once, his rifle in the crook of his arm. "Who is it?" he called out.

"It's me—Dan'l," came in a sleepy voice. "I just wanted"—he yawned hugely—"just wanted to see how the hosses were gettin' on." He rubbed some of the salve from his fingers onto the grass ostentatiously. Another yawn. "Sorry I woke you up."

The others, half-roused, grunted and returned to their sleep. Only Timothy had not stirred. Yet Daniel had seen the firelight shine on the slits of his half-opened eyes.

All during the following morning, Daniel tried to decide whether he should speak to Josiah about what he had seen. There was nothing wrong with it, perhaps. It was possible that Timothy had a friend who had settled in these parts, and who made a point of meeting him like this whenever the pack-horse train was due at Fort St. Clair. But there were so many holes in this idea that he soon discarded it.

Did Timothy have an Indian friend? Was he, perhaps, one of the Legion's spies, working in this way? None of these things sounded the right note to Daniel's troubled mind. And by afternoon it was too late.

Each man had a ration of bear meat and parched corn which he was to eat on the road that day, for they were anxious to cover the distance to Fort Greeneville, the place where their loads would be delivered. There they might, if they were lucky, have a glimpse of General Anthony Wayne himself. Henry's string was in the lead with Josiah, as always, in the forefront. Next came Simon's string, with Amos and Daniel behind him. Last of all were the injured ponies, driven by Timothy.

Ben was often with him, but Ben's job was to patrol the entire line. It was when he was in the van, talking to Josiah, that it happened.

There was a shout from the boys and Simon as Timothy's string broke loose and went racing into the forest at either side. "Stay here!" Amos shouted to Simon, and he and Daniel ran after the disappearing horses at full speed.

Daniel could hear Ben shouting farther on, and knew that he and Josiah had joined the search for the lost animals. Timothy was nowhere to be seen.

Once Daniel glimpsed one of the ponies in the distance. It was running free, the rope which normally tied it to its fellows flying in the wind. The rope did not look as if it had snapped. The end had been neatly severed.

He turned to tell Amos of what he had seen, but Amos was not there. Suddenly Daniel realized that he was alone in the forest, without a gun, without a companion, and that the troop was gone from sight and hearing.

His breath rasped in his throat—not from his running, but from stark fear. Which way had he come? Where were the others? For a moment sheer panic overcame him and he shouted wildly, hopelessly.

Josiah's voice reached him, bringing him to his senses like a shock of cold water. "Those hosses didn't break loose for nothin'," Josiah said, coming from the deep woods with an angry frown between his bright blue eyes. Even his beard seemed to bristle with anger. "Simon says mebbe a bear scairt them, but there's no sign of bear that *I* can see, and

63

the hosses in Simon's string and yours wasn't scairt, so what was it?"

Daniel said, still trembling from his fright, "I saw one of the hosses just now, and it looked to me like his lead rope had been cut."

"If you saw him, why didn't you catch him?" Josiah demanded.

"He was too far away," Daniel admitted.

"If he was too far away to catch, I'd think he was too far away to see a thing like that," Josiah snorted.

"But that's not all!" In his eagerness to justify his suspicions of Timothy, Daniel told his story wrong. "Timothy met a man in the woods last night—a stranger—and—"

"How do *you* know?" The gaze Josiah bent upon him was impatient and skeptical.

"I followed him when he got up from the campfire. Everybody else was asleep. Do you think—"

"I think," said Josiah harshly, "that you're imaginin' things. Do you expect me to believe you went wanderin' in the woods at dead of night, when you were so scairt right now in the daylight that you were hollerin' your head off?" He turned away in disgust, and Daniel, hating himself for his fear, would have liked to turn in the other direction, but dared not.

Of the string of ten, only two horses were caught. Josiah checked the loads with a wry twist to his mouth. "Flour and ammunition," he said. "You'll pay for this carelessness, Timothy," But Timothy, although he put on a show of distress, did not seem too disturbed.

All the way to Greeneville they had to hurry, for the mishap had made them late and they were determined to get to the fort before darkness fell. "Thank heaven it's summer, and stays light for a long time," Amos murmured.

"Does your pa run this pack-horse train in the winter, too?" Daniel asked, but his thoughts were elsewhere.

"No, it don't pay enough then. There's no forage for the hosses, so we'd have to carry their feed. A hoss'll eat a third of its load in feed."

Daniel was scarcely listening. Twice he opened his mouth to tell Amos his suspicions of Timothy, and twice he closed it again, for he dared not risk his new friend's scorn. If Mr. Gregg thought so poorly of him, Amos might think worse, for Amos was closer to him.

There was not too much breath for talking anyhow. Every bit of strength was needed to urge the tired animals onward, to see that they did not stray from the military road, to tighten insecure packs and girths, to watch out for tree stumps and mudholes.

When at last the pickets of the fort loomed in sight, Daniel drew a deep breath. Now he could rest; now there would be real safety for them all.

Josiah went to find the quartermaster to whom he was to deliver his supplies. The boys stood quietly by their animals, hot and tired and hungry, and Daniel thought to himself that at least this goal had been reached. He wondered how many goals there would be in his life to strive for, to attain, and, perhaps, to pass.

"That's him! Over there! Look!" Amos poked Daniel in the ribs so hard that it hurt.

"Who? Where?"

"Over *there!* Don't you see him? Old Toney himself!"

Daniel craned his neck to catch a glimpse of the tall, florid man who walked slowly and with a limp between two of his officers. He was disappointed, somehow. In his mind's eye, he had envisioned General Anthony Wayne as splendidly lithe, with classic features and hawks' eyes.

All he could find to say in his disappointment was, "I didn't know he was lame."

"It's the gout, Pa says. Pa says he's so lamed with it any other man would be in his bed and moanin' for the leech, but Old Toney don't let it get him down. He keeps an eye on everything, even if he has to be lifted up on his horse by his men."

Perhaps he did have hawks' eyes, then. The thought was consoling. After all, was not this the man who was to make the frontier safe from the Indians? If *he* failed, would not all the settlers who had braved the wilderness be doomed to failure, too?

The boys had not heard Ben come up behind them. "Know what the Indians call him?" Ben demanded suddenly. "No

66

Toney Lumpkins for them! They call him the Whirlwind. Or, sometimes, the Black Snake. That's what they think of him!"

"How do you know what they call him?" Amos asked. He grinned as he spoke. "You been makin' talk with any Indians around here?"

"Next best thing," Ben said laconically. "Spies."

"Spies?" Both boys spoke at once, and their eyes lighted with excitement. Like everyone else, they had heard of the wonderful work accomplished against the enemy by General Wayne's little band of trained men.

"D'you know Cap'n Kibby?" Daniel asked. "He's from Columbia."

"I know one of his men," Ben admitted. "He's been one of Kibby's rangers right along. But the big news is about Cap'n Wells and his latest catch."

His eyes twinkled as he saw how eager the boys were for his news. Captain Kibby's rangers went afoot as scouts for the army. But Captain Wells and the few men attached to his command lived like gentlemen in the encampment. They were privileged to take any horse from the dragoons that they might need for their assignments, and their exploits made fine telling around the campfires.

"Of course, you know that Cap'n Wells was brought up among the Indians. And so was Henry Miller, one of his men. Well, it seems Miller left a brother with the Indians when he turned white again—fellow by the name of Christopher who liked the Indian life too well to leave it.

"A few days back, Old Toney sent the cap'n out to bring back an Indian prisoner so's they could question him. They went away up along the Auglaize and there, on high ground, they surprised three Indians. Wells and Miller shot two of 'em, and McClellan, who can run circles around a deer when he's a mind to, took off after the third one. What does that Indian do but jump off a cliff into the river! The water was low and he sunk in the mud up to his middle and stuck there. Along comes McClellan, full speed, and jumps right in after him, mud or no mud. By the time Wells and Miller come up, McClellan had the Indian pretty well tamed."

Daniel shivered. "All by himself?"

"Sure. One white man against one Indian. Why not?" Ben stopped to laugh aloud, and added. "Only this time it weren't no Indian! When the others come up, and drug him out'n the river mud, and washed the war paint off'n him, he turned out to be a white man!"

"A renegade?" Amos asked. "Or a Britisher?"

"Neither. You'll scarce believe it when I tell you it was Henry Miller's brother Christopher that he hadn't see for months. At first the fellow wouldn't talk at all, but finally he admitted who he was. *And,*" Ben ended his story with a flourish, "he's right here at Fort Greeneville in the guardhouse this very minute, with his brother Henry and Cap'n Wells tryin' to git him to talk, and come over to our side."

"It don't seem possible a thing like that could happen," Amos said doubtfully.

Ben bridled a little, then laughed again. "If you don't believe me," he said, "ask anyone. The story's all over the place, and the latest word is that Christopher's weakenin'. Myself, I don't know whether I'd really trust a man that had been a white Indian ever since he was a lad."

"*Henry* Miller is trusted," Amos said quickly.

"Aye, but Henry Miller left the Indians of his own accord. And so did Cap'n Wells. This Christopher, now. . . . I don't know. . . ."

Daniel turned away. Wherever he went there was this talk about Indians. It was natural, of course, for the whole purpose of this string of forts, the whole reason for the Legion and the spies and the reconnoitering, was the eradication of the Indian menace. Twenty times a day he wished that he could have been living safely in some place like Cincinnati until the campaign was over. Yet even in Cincinnati there were plenty of Indian alarms, despite the protection of nearby Fort Washington. Why, matters had become so serious in the neighborhood that a number of men had banded together only last month to offer bounties for Indian scalps.

Was there no safety anywhere on the frontier?

CHAPTER SIX

Daniel had several more glimpses of General Anthony Wayne before they left Greeneville the following day. Each time he felt a greater confidence in the limping man. He could see how piercing the hazel eyes were, how strong the jaw. And the more stories he heard about him, the more his confidence grew. If anyone was going to defeat the Indians, it would be this man. There was a feeling of watchful power about him. Even the Indians believed that he never slept.

"He's a wily one," Daniel heard one soldier telling another. "The redskins never know which way *this* cat is goin' to jump. Look at the roads we've built for him! Goin' this-away and that, so's they've no way of guessin' which one we'll use when we march ag'in 'em. *We* don't know, neither!" His laugh was raucous.

Another time he overheard two men who were helping to unload and store the pack-horse-borne supplies. "Never know what's comin' next, we don't. Me, I never thought, when I took the bounty and joined the Legion, that I'd be buildin' roads and cuttin' through the forest one day, and yellin' my lungs out in bayonet practice the next. And here I am unloadin' supplies. I'd be willin' to bet you my boots it'll be somethin' else tomorrow or next week. Never know what Old Toney'll

Daniel had never seen anything like Fort Greeneville.

think up next!" But his voice held a note of pride. This was not a complaint.

Fort Greeneville itself held many marvels for Daniel. He had not seen its like before. Fort Washington had a more settled look with its covering of red paint. And it was located on the Ohio River, with the town of Cincinnati beside it. This was a great stockade enclosing fifty acres, in the midst of the wilderness. True, the location itself was a pleasant one, and a winding creek formed a natural moat on several sides. The prairie around it was large enough, Josiah said, to graze a thousand cattle. But it was in Indian country, and who knew what lay beyond that innocent-looking prairie?

It was obvious that General Wayne was taking no chances of a surprise attack. The soldiers' huts were surrounded by a deep trench, with a raised fire-step inside them for defense against attack. And there was the stockade itself. If anything could withstand a powerful Indian onslaught, it would be this place. Daniel wished with all his heart that the troop could have made its camp inside its safe walls, rather than in the exposed position the men had to take outside.

He ventured a remark or two about this, but Amos only grinned. "Shucks, Dan'l, you don't think any Indians could sneak across that prairie to us without bein' seen, do you? We'd have all the time we needed to git inside the fort afore they could reach us. Old Toney's got plenty of sentries in the nighttime, so rest easy." He put his hand on Daniel's shoulder in a brief gesture of reassurance and affection, and Daniel's heart swelled with gratitude. Amos, at least, did not despise him for his ever-present fear.

They started back the next morning. With most of Timothy's string gone, the big man was told to help Simon. The going was easier without the loads that the animals had carried on the trip up and they made good time to Fort St. Clair, camping early that first night. Henry was sent out to get the meat for them, and came back in a short while with a fine bag of raccoon, pheasants, and a couple of rabbits.

Simon, who shone as the cook, made a savory stew for them, and then they all sat around the campfire and talked a while before they lay down to sleep.

"I'm surprised you didn't come back with a bear, Henry," Josiah said, pretending to scoff at Henry's hunting prowess. "Dan'l got us a bear when we stopped here on the way up. Your eyesight failin' any?"

"Oh, I saw a couple of bears—some buffalo, too—but I didn't want the bother of toting them back here," Henry said with a grin. "No use killing the animals just for the sport. I thought you wanted something Simon could cook in a hurry."

Amos leaned over to whisper to Daniel, "Henry is the best shot I ever saw. He can drive a nail into a tree at fifty paces."

Daniel's eyes widened. Henry was the silent one who kept to himself most of the time. He carried a book or two in his personal bundle, which he would take out to read whenever he had time. Henry had not seemed to Daniel to be the sort of man who would be an outstanding shot.

Simon said slowly, "Don't see many buffalo any more. When I first come into the Territory, they was plenty."

"They've moved west," Henry said. "First the buffalo, then the Indians, then the other big game will disappear. That's the way it will be as men come in and settle."

"You seem pretty sure of the Indians goin'," Timothy sneered. "Might be it'll be us that leaves."

"No, I don't think so." Henry's voice was quiet, sure. "The Indians are wanderers. They follow the game. Even their villages and cornfields are temporary, if you look at them from the standpoint of years of time. When one area has been stripped of its game, they will leave their villages and go on to some other place where the game is plentiful. . . . But the white man comes to settle permanently. He wants to build a home, to clear fields and plant crops with the idea of staying there, of leaving property to his children. He wants to put down roots for his family. When he fights, he is not fighting for an indefinite hunting area, but for a certain farm, an acreage that is his. And so he will fight harder and longer than the Indians."

Josiah said, "You're right, Henry. My folks have always moved on from place to place, lookin' for a spot to settle where they could have plenty, where they could be free, and where they could think of their families goin' on and on. I know that's what I've found where I've settled now. I want my children to have what I've worked for, because I think it's better here than anywheres else my folks have tried it."

Daniel saw Amos' surprised expression and knew that this was the first time the boy had heard his father say this. For some reason, it gave him a feeling of relief. From the time he had first seen the Greggs' farm and met the family, he had hated to think that their fine acreage and sturdy house would hold them only temporarily. Even though they might spend years on the place, if there was always the possibility of moving on, it could never be what he had sensed it should be—a true outpost of civilization.

The thoughts that sped through his mind were unformed, but the relief was there, and he could see from Amos' relaxed posture that he, too, was glad to hear his father speak that way.

Timothy broke the brief silence. "Better here?" he repeated, with a faint sneer. "What have you got here in the Territory but work—and too much of it? You'll not grow rich! What if you *was* to raise the biggest crops in the country? What'll you do with 'em? You can eat only so much. Where are you goin' to find a market for the rest?"

"I figger that by the time my crops are that big," Josiah said with a slow smile, "there'll be ways of gettin' rid of 'em. I can always cart 'em to the Miami and flatboat 'em down river to Cincinnati. And from there to New Orleans, mebbe."

Timothy snorted. "How you goin' to sell your corn, or your hogs, for that matter? In the ear, and on the hoof?"

"By that time," Josiah said with assurance, "we'll have mills to make flour, and we'll be able to salt down the pork."

"Not with salt costin' what it does today," Timothy shot back.

"No, 'course not. But when the country gets more settled, and when I'll have the hogs to kill, salt will be down within reason, too. You wait and see."

"I'll wait," Timothy growled, "but I'm bettin' I won't see any of it."

They turned in for the night then. Daniel lay awake for a half hour, pondering on what he had heard. In his mind, Josiah Gregg took the part of all serious-minded settlers, while Timothy represented those men—and there were many of them—who had no homes and wanted none, who went only where there was the chance to make a little money, who had no ties of any kind.

He knew instinctively that it was men like Mr. Gregg who would make this Ohio country into a true part of the United States. They would tame the forest, and build roads and mills and flatboats, and schools and churches before they were through. In a brief flash of perception, he saw what the future could be like. But first—the thought returned to him as it had so many times—first there was the Indian menace to overcome.

They were up early next morning, but had a hard time to find several of the pack-horses. Relieved now of their heavy loads in the daytime, the animals were less tired at night. They were inclined to stray farther in search of juicy grasses, despite their hickory hobbles.

"If you ask me, animals can be just as contrary as people," Henry said with a wry smile when they had finally rounded up the entire train, and were about to start out.

"All critters can be contrary," Josiah said, "and if you was to take up farmin', you'd find that plants can be the same. As for weather—" He cast a look up at the sky. "No need to go further than today. Cool and pleasant when we got up, and already it's hot enough to fry hog cracklin's on the road."

It was true. The day had turned unbearably hot, and as soon as they had left the clearing around the fort and had set out on the road to Fort Hamilton, the closeness of the forest seemed to reach out for them. Daniel broke into a sweat every time he had to run along the line to examine the ponies, and when he helped Amos tighten a girth, he puffed and panted. So did Amos.

"Whew! If we don't git a storm to blow away this heat, there ain't goin' to be enough of me left to fill my moccasins," Amos said. "I'll be all melted down. I don't know *when* we've had it like this."

Timothy kept up a continual rumble of complaint, and once Amos whispered to Daniel, "It don't seem like he'd know enough cuss words to make it sound different by this time, but he always comes up with some new ones!"

Daniel grinned. "I reckon he's so busy thinkin' up things to say about the heat, it keeps his mind off how hot he is."

His linsey-woolsey shirt prickled, and his deerskin leggings were uncomfortably warm. When he tried to whistle, he found his lips were too parched to pucker properly. But the men had to hurry to make up the time they had spent hunting for the horses.

Just before noon they rounded a bend in the road and saw another pack-horse train coming toward them. The leader, a swarthy, bowlegged man with lank hair and a long upper lip, stopped briefly to talk with Josiah. It was apparent that the two knew each other. Daniel listened unashamedly.

"Had a good trip up?" Josiah asked the man.

"Not bad."

"Pretty hot today, ain't it?"

"Yup."

"Anything to watch out for on the trail?" Josiah persevered.

"Couple trees down two miles back."

"Any sign of Indians?" Daniel held his breath at this.

"Yup."

Now Josiah's interest quickened. "You see any?" he said quickly.

"Not me. Express scalped, though, near the fort yestiddy."

Josiah frowned. "An express scalped near the fort! How near?"

"Other side o' the river, 'bout two mile. Still warm when they found him. Pigs was lappin' up the blood. Still fresh."

Despite the heat, Daniel shuddered violently. His breath came short. There was still time to turn back to the safety of Fort St. Clair. Surely Mr. Gregg wouldn't go on in the face of this news?

"Hmmm." Josiah was thoughtful. "We got a late start, but I reckon we can make it to Fort Hamilton before night."

"Keep an eye out," the other man said, and prepared to move on.

There was a chorus of salutations from the various pack-horse drivers as the two trains passed each other and then the silence of the forest overtook them once more. Josiah wasn't going to turn back.

Daniel felt as if his eyes and ears were sticking out from his head in his effort to see everything and hear everything which might be out of the ordinary. But there was nothing to see and nothing to hear. The countryside seemed completely uninhabited.

They ate their noon meal without stopping, and Amos said, "We're mighty short on meat. I wonder if we'll have time this evening—" He did not finish the sentence.

The sun was high in the heavens when Timothy reported that several of the horses were lame. His two horses had been added to Simon's string. "Always your string that has trouble, ain't it?" Josiah said with a grim look. "Well, we'll have to go slower, that's all." He examined the two, and heaved a sigh. "I'd hate to lose 'em. They're good ponies."

78

Daniel whispered to Amos, "But how'll we make it to the fort if we go slower?"

"We won't," Amos said. "We'll have to camp somewheres."

Daniel thought back to the evening at the Worders' when Mr. Reese had suggested he join a pack-horse troop. What a fool he had been to leave the comparative safety of that farm! And yet, once he had heard what Mr. Worder said to the stranger, he had had to go.

But couldn't he have chosen some other work to do—something that would have kept him in Cincinnati, where there was at least the protection of Fort Washington? Then he shook his head, answering himself silently. What did a twelve-year-old lad have to offer? He had no trade. He could neither read nor write, although he had always thought it might be interesting to learn how someday. He was not too tall; he was not especially strong. He was, to most people, simply another mouth to feed. He should be glad that he had had the chance to work for Mr. Gregg.

Well, he told himself, he *was* glad, but that didn't keep him from having the gizzard scared right out of him most of the time. They would have to camp tonight only a few miles from where the express had been scalped yesterday. What if people did say that the time you were safest from the Indians was right after an attack! Then they would have fled away from possible pursuit.

But this wasn't right after the attack, this was a day and a half later. By now the Indians might have come back, looking for more scalps. His own grew cold at the thought.

"The heat gettin' you?" Amos asked him, after one look at his pale face.

"No," Daniel said slowly, thinking he might as well tell the truth. "I'm afeared, that's all."

"Well," Amos said kindly, trying to encourage him, "if you can say 'that's all,' then you ain't *too* scairt!"

CHAPTER SEVEN

The night passed without incident other than a thunderstorm. Daniel was surprised next morning to find that he had slept well. This cheered him immensely, and he was whistling merrily when he and Amos rounded up their string of horses in the woods. For the first time, he forgot to think about the Indians.

"Pa says we're goin' to stop by home for a look-in," Amos said. He, too, was feeling cheerful at the prospect of seeing his mother and brothers and sisters again.

"Now?" Daniel asked. "Afore we git to Cincinnati?"

"That's right. It'll be right nice to have a bite of Ma's cookin', too."

"Might be she won't have time to make anythin'," Daniel said cautiously, "if she's not expectin' us."

"But she is!" Amos said. "Pa says he told her he'd stop by and pick up Polly to take along to the town. She's to visit Aunt Lydia till we come back, and buy some things Ma wants in the stores."

This was the first Daniel had heard of it. He was happy to think he would see more of the Gregg family, and especially Polly who had been so kind to him. But he was shy, too. Shyer than he would have been if he had not felt so grateful to all of them for their kindness to him.

They paused briefly at Fort Hamilton on their way, so as not to lose any time, for it would be a long trip this day. Almost at once, Daniel was aware of a different air about the fort. The men wore gloomy faces, and there was more than one who had a hangdog look about him. They came out to greet the pack-horse train, but Daniel noticed that none of them ventured very far from the fort.

"You heard the news?" one of them asked Josiah.

"About the express? Yes, we heard it."

"Terrible thing, wasn't it? He must ha' been kilt right after he left here. Hardly got across the river, they say. Goes to show they're all about us."

"Who are?" Josiah's voice held a stern note.

"The Indians! Why, I haven't slept a wink since. Got a family livin' here outside the fort, but if those varmints can sneak down on folks that quick and that quiet, they'd never have a chance to make it to the gate in time. I'd lose my cow, too, I reckon."

Josiah said heartily, "I've a family of my own, livin' a few miles south of here. They have no fort nearby to run to. But I don't worry about them—too much. That's one of the things we took on when we moved out here—the chance of Indians, just like there's the chance of a drought, or a flood. You have to wait till it comes, and then fight it. Worryin' about it ahead of time don't get you nowheres."

Mr. Gregg was right, of course. Daniel knew that, but he knew, too, that it wasn't as easy as it sounded to look at things the way Mr. Gregg did. Still, it was comforting to be with someone who felt that way. Some of his confidence was bound to rub off onto you.

They pushed on to the Greggs' homestead clearing, and this time Daniel was able to see the place in the full morning light. The dogs heard them when they were still far down the rutted lane, and ran barking and leaping to greet their master. The twins came pelting after them, and Josiah caught them both, one in each powerful arm, and lifted them up in greeting.

By the time they reached the house, Mrs. Gregg was standing smiling in the doorway, holding little Sabrina, and Polly stood by her side, the sun's rays caught in her tawny hair.

At first she tried to be dignified, as befitted a young lady, but she was unable to restrain herself, and rushed to her father with a squeal of pleasure. He swung her high, too, her braids flying in an arc. "Ready to come with us?" he boomed. "We've not long to stay. We couldn't make it to Fort Hamilton last night, so we're late today."

His eyes sought his wife's questioning ones, and he said, more soberly, "Two of the horses went lame, and I'm leavin' them here. Then, when we heard there'd been a scalpin' near the fort, we thought it wiser to make camp than to travel in the dark."

His words had added meaning. He said, after a brief pause, "I thought I might leave Henry here with you and the childern. I'll pick him up on my next trip. That is, if Henry's willin'."

"Glad to stay," Henry said. "Maybe I'll get a bit of reading done, if Mrs. Gregg doesn't wear me out with chores!" He laughed as he spoke, and Josiah and his wife laughed, too. It was clear that Henry was an old friend of the family and would be welcome.

"I'm ready, Pa," Polly said. She spoke breathlessly, and Daniel could see that she was excited, for her color was deep under her freckles. "I've got my bundle ready, and Ma has told me over and over what she wants, and what I'm to tell Aunt Lydia."

Mrs. Gregg insisted that they take along some corn dodger she had baked the day before, and gave them each a generous slab of her homemade cheese. Polly was mounted on one of the ponies atop a pad of blankets, a small bundle clutched in one hand. A venison ham, a bunch of dried herbs, and a large cheese, all destined for Aunt Lydia, were tied to the packsaddle of one of the ponies. The children waved and shouted as long as the pack-horse train was in sight.

There was not much chance to talk on the way to Cincinnati. Because they had farther to go than usual, they saved their breath for the trip. Once Polly, who was riding with Amos' string, called out to her brother, "Did you get to see Gen'l Wayne this trip?"

Amos answered, "Tell you all about it when we stop to eat."

But there was no chance to tell much when they did stop, for the horses had to be allowed to graze, and there was only time for a few hasty bites of the corn dodger and cheese before Josiah gave the signal to go on again.

Polly's eyes were wide at the amount of traffic on the road, and once she commented on it. "Seems like we're meetin' a lot of people," she said. "Must be half of Cincinnati on the road today, and all runnin' supply trains."

Daniel was near her when she spoke, and he laughed. "The nearer we get to town, the more we meet," he agreed. "But some of the supplies get left at Fort Hamilton, and still more at St. Clair. By the time you get to the road between St.

Clair and Jefferson, there's big lonely stretches where you don't meet nobody."

She accepted his explanation, but shook her head. "Still, it hardly looks like there'll be anybody left in Cincinnati."

"It's gettin' to be a big place. Your pa says there's more than six hunnerd people livin' there. That's pretty big. Gettin' bigger all the time, too, with folks comin' from the east in a steady stream."

"It's a city!" Polly cried. "I don't think I'd like to live in a place as crowded as that, do you?"

Daniel hesitated. There would be safety in a crowd, wouldn't there? Polly seemed to read his mind, and said quickly, "Look at what happened last year when there was smallpox rampagin' all around. They say Cincinnati lost a third of its folks!" She added slyly, "That's more'n the Indians ever kilt off. And it was so quick, too."

Daniel pondered her words for a long time. He had not thought about it in quite that way, but it was true that if you looked at it like this, smallpox was more to be feared than the Indians. Yet he was not afraid of smallpox, and never had been. Perhaps because he had never lived in a family where it struck.

That thought brought another to the forefront of his mind. Suppose he *had* lived unscathed through a smallpox epidemic, would he have been as terrified of the disease ever afterward as he was now of the Indians? In other words, was he a coward who would always be smitten with fear of whatever danger had menaced him in the past? He did not think so, yet how could he be sure?

85

When they reached Cincinnati, their first duty was to get the animals to the spot where they usually camped, to remove the packsaddles, and feed the horses. Josiah went at once, although it was late in the afternoon, to see about the next consignment he was to carry to Greeneville, and delegated Amos and Daniel to accompany Polly to her Aunt Lydia's.

Aunt Lydia lived in a small frame house, which impressed Daniel mightily for it was usually only the wealthy who could afford frame rather than log construction for their homes. She was married to a man named Peter Torrence; he was a trader and had gone with some flatboats to New Orleans, so that, for the present, she was alone.

"Hasn't she any children?" Daniel asked, not sure whether he should inquire into something so personal, yet anxious to know.

"They all died," Amos said in a matter-of-fact way. "Some from the ague, and two from the smallpox last year. She's not like Ma at all, though she's her sister. She's tall and thin, and she's got a right tart tongue at times."

"Well, she's had troubles to try her," Polly said. "Might be you'd have a tart tongue, too, if you'd been through what she has!"

Daniel hung back while Polly and her brother were greeted by their aunt, but then Polly called to him, and he brought the gifts of food which Mrs. Gregg had sent her sister.

"This is Dan'l," Polly said, taking his hand with a proprietary air. "He's workin' for Pa right now, but when the Indians have been beat, he's goin' to live with us."

Daniel flushed with pleasure. "It's right kind of you and

86

Amos to say that," he said hurriedly, "but your ma and pa might feel different about it."

Polly looked indignant. "Why would they? You haven't any folks, and we've plenty of room. You'd be workin' for Pa, same as you are now, only it'd be work on the farm, that's all."

Aunt Lydia turned a piercing gaze upon him. "He's not as strong-lookin' as you, Amos," she said.

"He's not as old as I am, neither," Amos said casually. "He'll fill out with Ma's cookin' in a couple years. He's strong enough for his age and size."

Daniel backed away then, to stand with the horse's reins in his hand, and in a short while Amos joined him. "They're goin' to the stores in the mornin'," he said. "Polly says Ma has a list a mile long of things she needs. Haven't seen so many traders out our way these days. Guess they're scairt of the Indians."

They went back to the encampment by way of Front Street —the street that ran above the river. Here most of the stores and taverns were clustered. A burst of raucous song came from one of the taverns as they paused, and a heavy figure lurched out. Amos drew Daniel to a stop.

"Timothy," he said in disgust. "Spendin' his money already. Pa pays him plenty, but he won't have a penny left by tomorrow, and what'll he do then? Pa says he's not goin' to hire him again. He's lazy, and careless, and don't care how many lies he tells."

Daniel was relieved. He had never liked the man, and ever since he had watched that strange meeting in the woods at night, he had wondered about him. Could he be a spy for the

British? On impulse, he told the story to Amos. But Amos, like his father, looked doubtful.

"You think he sold his hosses to somebody—British or Indian, it don't matter—that night? And then let 'em loose the next day?" He shook his head. "Why'd he damage 'em then beforehand? It don't make sense."

Daniel said eagerly, "Mebbe that was just his usual carelessness. Mebbe he didn't want 'em sore—they just got that way because he didn't load 'em right. Or mebbe he hurt 'em a-purpose so's he wouldn't be suspected. So folks'd think just what you're thinkin' now."

Amos still shook his head. "Well, they're gone, and Pa took a real loss on 'em. But I still don't think. . . . How'd they know where he was a-goin' to cut 'em loose, if what you think is true? Tell me that!"

Daniel said, with a shudder, "If they was Indians, they could have followed alongside of us in the woods, and we wouldn't have seen 'em. Then, as soon as the hosses were cut loose—and I'd swear that rope had been cut, Amos—they were run off and hid from us."

"The ropes on the two we caught could ha' been broken, not cut," Amos said.

Amos was still doubtful, Daniel could see, and he began to wonder if he was unduly suspicious, or whether Amos and his father were too trusting. When they got to their camp, Simon was nowhere to be seen, and Ben was waiting for them impatiently.

"Here, you lads, take care of the hosses. Your pa needs me, Amos, and I've got to git along. Dan'l, Mr. Gregg says you're to have a reg'lar string of your own next trip—you did so well helpin' Amos this time, he says he feels he can trust you with a small one. He's out buyin' ponies right now. Saddles, too, if he can git 'em."

Daniel's chest felt tight with emotion. This was something he had not expected. To think that Mr. Gregg thought so highly of him! He could not even stammer his appreciation, for his throat had closed up. But Amos clapped him on the back and said, "There, now! You're as good as a man, see?"

Daniel blinked back sudden tears and said, "I'll work hard. See if I don't! Your pa won't be sorry, Amos."

They spent the whole next day in Cincinnati and since Simon, poorer and soberer than he had been the day before, had no more money to spend, he was left with the horses while Amos and Daniel saw the town. Daniel, of course, had no gun, and it was his ambition to own one, so first they looked at guns. There were muskets and rifles. Daniel gazed longingly at a slim, long-barreled rifle with a fine walnut stock, but did not even dare to ask the price. He knew it would be a long time before he could afford a gun like that.

Next, they went to get new moccasins. The footgear they had worn on the march was worn thin and would not last for many more miles of such rough wear. After that, Amos said he was going to buy his mother a present—a loaf of sugar.

Daniel was aghast at the thought of such extravagance. "You've got maple sweetenin' at home," he reminded Amos. "And the Worders used to boil down punkins for a kind of molasses. Loaf sugar's only for rich folks."

"Yes, but Ma said once she wished she had some. She said

if she had, she'd make us some sweet cakes like she used to back in Pennsylvania. And I'd sure like to sink a tooth into some of those again!"

Daniel laughed. "So that's the real reason!"

They went into the store of Findlay and Smith, and instantly Daniel was amazed. So many things for sale; so many unusual things. He wondered where there could be a market for all of them. There were kegs of wines and liquors, tobacco and "segars," coffee, tea, and chocolate among the luxuries. There were bolts of nankeen and cambric and linen, hair ribbons and pomades, and blackball for polishing boots.

His head was whirling at the sight of all these things for sale, and he was just about to ask Amos who could be the buyers of such merchandise, when he heard Polly's voice behind him. He turned around, and found she was half-hidden by her Aunt Lydia.

"I want some needles," she was saying, "both heavy and fine." She was clutching an iron kettle by the handle. It was new, and already held other purchases.

"Isn't that heavy?" Daniel asked. He saw her head jerk back with surprise.

"I told you to set it on the floor, Polly," Aunt Lydia said. "Ain't nobody goin' to steal it from you."

Polly flushed a little and set the pot on the floor. When Amos later bought the sugar loaf for his mother, that went into the pot, too. There were all kinds of things in it but, as Daniel said with a laugh, "wouldn't none of 'em make a good stew."

Polly carried the kettle when they left the shop. It was customary for a woman to carry her own bundles, and she felt she was nearly a woman, Daniel could see. She walked proudly beside her aunt, skirting mud puddles and scuffing through the dirt in her best, and only, pair of shoes. Amos and Daniel, staring at all the sights of the water front, soon dropped behind.

It was Aunt Lydia's voice that brought them on the run. "Get away from me!" she was shouting. "You rude louts! Get away!"

Daniel, racing toward them, saw that a couple of rowdies had swaggered out of one of the taverns and were blocking Aunt Lydia's and Polly's path. When they moved to the right, the men followed suit. When they moved to the left, the men dodged over that way, too. As Daniel came near he heard one of them say, "What you got in that kettle? Somethin' good? Somethin' *I'd* like?" And with the words, he snatched the pot out of Polly's hands and fled.

Polly, without a moment's hesitation, ran after him, and so did her aunt. But the other ruffian successfully headed off Aunt Lydia, and the thief, with Polly at his heels, suddenly rounded on her and knocked her to the ground.

Anger made a red haze in front of Daniel's eyes. The delay had been just long enough to allow him to catch up with them, and now he launched himself upon the man with such force that the two of them were borne to the ground. The kettle clattered as it fell and the numerous parcels flew out in all directions.

In the next few seconds of furious wrestling, Daniel remembered everything he had ever heard about the fighters on the

Cincinnati water front—the tales of eye-gouging, nose-biting, ear-chewing, and bone-breaking all flashed before him and, in some miraculous fashion, he managed to keep out of his opponent's grasp.

That time was all he needed, for Amos had reached him by then, and with two strong young lads upon him, both wildly furious, the man decided to turn tail and run. His companion went pounding after him.

Polly was already on her feet, her eyes blazing, a long smudge of dust along one cheek, and her dress dirty and rumpled. "The bully!" she cried. "Oh, I wish I could have been a man to give him what he deserved!" Then her eyes softened, and she smiled at them. "But it was the next best thing to watch how the two of you handled him!" She tossed her head proudly.

Aunt Lydia came up, chattering with rage, and darting right and left to retrieve the bundles that had been in the pot. Polly and the boys helped her, and soon they were on their way again. It had all happened so quickly that the few onlookers had had no time to intervene.

Walking back to Aunt Lydia's house, Daniel knew a lightness of heart that had not been his for several years. It was almost like having a family of his own to be so close to Amos and Polly and all the other Greggs. Even Aunt Lydia looked handsomer and kindlier to him because she belonged to them.

Suddenly he wanted to burst into song, but did not dare. His voice was too much inclined these days to go from treble to bass without warning. And so he hummed a little instead, an old song his father had often sung.

"Feelin' chipper, ain't you?" Aunt Lydia said, but her sour

Daniel launched himself upon the thief.

tone was belied by her smile. "Well, day after tomorrow you head back into the Indian country again, so you might as well be cheerful now."

But not even the mention of Indians could dampen Daniel's spirits.

CHAPTER EIGHT

They were ready to leave the Gregg farm two days later when Daniel suddenly called Polly to him. "I near forgot," he said, flushing red with embarrassment. "I wanted to give you this afore we go. I—I don't own anythin' else you might want." He thrust the pewter button that had been his father's into her warm hand and turned away quickly. But Polly ran after him.

"Where'd you get it?" she asked, highly pleased with his gift.

"It was Pa's. It was on his coat. It must have got torn off when the Indians grabbed it, because the coat wasn't there any more when I—when I found him. I hid it for the whole time I was with the Worders. Just so's I'd have something that was mine, you see."

"But now"—her face wore an expression of real distress—"now you won't have anythin' at all!"

"I've got me a job—a real one," he said proudly. "I'll be able to buy things now if I need 'em. . . . But that's not the reason I wanted you to have it," he added. "It's because I thought so much of it. It's been like a little bit of magic. I always felt, when I had it, that nothin' would harm me."

Polly's smile lighted her whole face, "Why, Dan'l," she cried, "I think it's right sweet of you to want me to have it! I hope it keeps on bein' magical for me, too."

"It will," he said earnestly. "I'm certain-sure."

He did not stop to think that it was odd he no longer felt the need of it himself; this did not occur to him. He heard Josiah's hallooing signal for the start and got his horses into line. Soon the clustered Gregg family and the cabin were lost to view.

There was another haying detail in the prairie below Fort Hamilton. The fort itself no longer looked as large to Daniel as it had the first time he saw it, now that he had visited Fort Greeneville. That afternoon they passed the taciturn pack-horse master who had told them about the scalping near Fort Hamilton. He was on his return trip and would be in Cincinnati by evening. Already Daniel was beginning to know and to recognize many of the men who drove the pack-horse trains.

The following day was uneventful, with only moderate showers in the afternoon. "I wish we'd have a reg'lar slam-bang thunderstorm to clear the air," Amos complained as they made camp that evening outside Fort St. Clair. "It's so close I could cut it with my knife."

Daniel said, thoughtfully, "If I'd had any sense, I'd have bought a better knife than this in Cincinnati." He looked with disfavor at the cheap one he had purchased. "But I thought I was savin' money not to. I reckon my pa was right. He used to say that buyin' cheap things was givin' good money for bad goods."

"I'll hone it for you," Simon offered. His own hunting knife was razor-sharp. " 'Course I don't guarantee it'll *keep* an edge, but leastways I'll put an edge to it."

Daniel was grateful. That night, after their simple supper, Simon sat by the fire and patiently whetted the cheap knife until it was reasonably sharp. With it hanging in the sheath from his belt, and with the musket Josiah had lent him for the trip, Daniel felt well armed.

Soon they turned in, lying close, but not too close, to the dying fire, and Daniel stretched out, shielding his eyes from the light with his arms. He was full of a new content. In what a short time he had progressed from a penniless, unwanted lad to one with responsibility, pay, and friends. There was still danger, of course, and there were times, every day, when his breath stood still at some untoward sound or the half-seen flight of a bird in the woods—anything which might have been an Indian. But he was always able to reassure himself, and the knowledge that he was with others who were brave and dependable soon restored his confidence.

Well, not all of them, he amended the thought. Not Timothy. For Timothy, to Daniel's distress, was with them again. Daniel knew that Josiah had not intended to engage the man again. He had paid him off at Cincinnati and had promptly looked for someone else to take his place. But there had been no one. This was the time when the contractors for the Legion were eager to get anyone they could, and pack-horse drivers were not to be found. Mr. Gregg had had to hire Timothy again.

He had not given him command of a string, however. Timothy had been told to stay at the head of Henry's string, for Henry had more to handle on this trip than any of the others. It was surprising how quick and efficient the quiet, scholarly Henry could be. Daniel doubted if Timothy was much help to him.

As if thought of the man had conjured him up, Daniel saw Timothy rise stealthily from his place near the fire. He gave a hurried look around, but Daniel's face was hidden by his arm. With a tread that was surprisingly silent for one of his bulk, Timothy had started to move away from the others when Daniel said, quite loudly, "Something the matter, Timothy?"

The man stopped short with a smothered curse. Josiah and Ben sat up at once, and Henry, who slept with his rifle in the crook of his arm, was not far behind them.

"Where you goin', Timothy?" Josiah asked.

Timothy stamped his foot. "Got a cramp in my leg," he answered in a surly voice. "Near drivin' me crazy, so I thought I'd git up and see if walkin' around would help."

It was a plain lie, to Daniel, for he had seen with what sure stealth Timothy had risen and moved, but he said nothing, for Josiah's doubt was obvious. He said dryly, "I think it'll get better if you stay here with us, Timothy. Might be you'd git an Indian arrow or a bullet in it that would be worse'n a cramp."

Timothy came back to the circle, limping heavily, and after he had crouched down by the fire he rubbed his leg for a while. Then, grunting with repressed anger, he lay down again.

Daniel went to sleep almost at once. He knew, without another word having been said, that he need not keep watch, that Josiah and the others would now be sleeping lightly in case Timothy tried to leave the circle again. And he knew, too, that Josiah was remembering what Daniel had told him about Timothy's other excursion at night into the woods. It was no coincidence that it should have happened again at their encampment outside Fort St. Clair.

The next day, too, he saw that Josiah and Ben took turns keeping close to Timothy, so that he had no chance to make a move of any kind without being seen. There would be no opportunity today to cut the rope of any of the pack-horses.

They made such good time that they had a longer rest at mid-day than usual. They sat together talking, and Amos and Daniel listened to the older men eagerly, for the talk turned, as always, upon the coming campaign.

"Seems like Gen'l Wayne could ha' licked the Indians last fall, 'stead of spendin' all his time buildin' Fort Greeneville," Simon said, chewing thoughtfully on a piece of cold venison.

"Why, when he and the Legion left Hobson's Choice last October, everybody thought sure he'd be up in Indian country in no time, with these wide roads and all. And what does he do? He stops where the wide road ends and builds another fort, and sets there all winter—except for buildin' Fort Recovery. All spring, too. An' he's *still* there!"

Everyone looked surprised, for Simon, slow and dull-witted as a rule, seldom opened his mouth for more than a sentence or two. It was apparent that this was something he had been thinking about for some time.

Henry said patiently, "But don't you see, Simon, he's done the wisest thing possible? What did General Harmar do? And General St. Clair? They marched north in the fall—both of them—and met the Indians and got beaten. The reasons weren't simple, but some of the reasons were that they did not have good roads for the army and supplies, and they did not have the support of stout forts upon the way, and they did not have an army that had been drilled and drilled until it was able to stand up against the enemy."

"Hmp!" said Timothy, with his mouth full. "Wayne's got the roads, and the forts, and the drilled army, but *he* ain't beat the Indians yet, neither!"

"Well, he will," Josiah said positively. "If ever I was certain-sure of anythin', it's that! He will!"

"That's only talk," Timothy protested. "Has he made any move to fight those Indians yet? Not he! He's gone on buildin' roads and forts, and drillin' the daylights out'n the men, and that's all."

"It will pay off in the end," Henry said. "He's wise to put so many spies to good use, and he's wise to want everything ready and right on his side before he risks his men in a fight. That way, he's almost sure to win. There won't be any happenstance about it when *he* marches against the Indians."

"I could wish there wasn't so much talk about trouble amongst his officers," Josiah said with a frown. "From the stories I hear, you'd think they was all scratchin' each others' eyes out, except when they're all tryin' to scratch out Gen'l Wayne's. That's a thing I don't like."

"General Scott is coming up from Kentucky with volunteers. He's a friend of Wayne's."

"Yeah, but they're militia. Might be they're not dependable in a pinch," Timothy sneered.

Simon bristled a little, and tucked his chin in, to glare at Timothy. "They're Kentucky militia," he said slowly, "an' that means they're the best fighters Wayne'll git."

"Time to move on," Ben said quickly. Daniel was sure he said it to avert a real argument.

Fort Greeneville was crowded, even more crowded than it had been before. Amos and Daniel wandered through the huge enclosure, staring at the soldiers' huts, at the washerwomen working near the spring, at the busy blacksmith's forge, at the fine house where the general was quartered. Soldiers were having bayonet practice at one end of the parade ground, dragoons were currying their horses, cook-fires were lighted. It was like a city in miniature.

A swarthy man rode through the gate and over to the general's house. Daniel clutched at Amos. "That's an Indian!" he cried. "And he's a-goin'—"

A soldier nearby turned to grin at them. "Sure, that's an Indian. He's a Chickasaw named Jemmy Underwood, and he's one of Captain Gibson's spies, over to Fort Recovery. We've got Indians workin' with us as well as ag'in us. I reckon Jemmy's here with dispatches for Old Toney."

Daniel's fear subsided somewhat. He said, "Last time we were here, Cap'n Wells and his men had brought in an Indian. Only it wasn't an Indian, really."

"You mean Christopher Miller?" the soldier said.

"That's the one. He was in the guardhouse, and folks said they were tryin' to get him to work for the Gen'l."

"Well, he didn't want to at first," the soldier told them. "But his brother and Cap'n Wells kep' at him, and Old Toney himself would go and talk to him. He didn't hold out too long. He's workin' for us now, an' they say he's right good at it."

"How could anyone rather stay an Indian if he was really a white man?" Daniel said slowly.

Amos answered him. "I can see that," he said. "If the Indians decide to adopt a boy into their family, they treat him fine. And so he grows up like one of 'em. Just think," he chuckled and poked Daniel in the ribs, "no farm chores to do—the Indian women do all that work—and nothin' to do all day but hunt and fish and play ball and jaw with your friends. Wouldn't you like that kind of life, Dan'l?"

"Not if I had to live with the Indians to get it," Daniel said with emphasis.

There was no glimpse to be had of the general this time. Rumor had it that he was ill with the gout again, an affliction that never really left him, and from which he suffered greatly. Somehow, Daniel realized, as they started their southward journey, he had missed seeing that tall, commanding figure very much. He hoped that on their next trip he would see him again.

For he was quite sure now that he would be employed for the next trip up, and for all the other trips to follow. He had never worked so hard in his life, but neither had he had such pleasure in his work before. And with every day, despite the physical weariness which weighed him down by evening, he knew he was growing stronger and more self-reliant. More of a man.

They passed several supply trains that day, more than they had ever passed before. They were large ones, with escorts of foot soldiers and dragoons to protect them from the Indians.

"The gen'l's pilin' up rations, and that's a sign things are goin' to move soon," Ben said.

The heavy wagons creaked by, and the horses neighed at one another, and the men saluted casually.

"Anythin' new at Fort St. Clair?" Simon called out.

"Nope," they answered.

No news was good news, and the pack-horse train hurried on, eager to stop for the night.

The road was beginning to be familiar now to Daniel. He could remember certain landmarks easily, and others were being impressed upon his memory without any effort on his part. The spots where it was boggy, and they had to go carefully, lest one of the horses fall into a hole and break a leg; the fords at the creeks; the wide, sunny, prairielike meadows; the dark stretches of heavy forest.

Sometimes they would come to a place where some past hurricane had felled hundreds of trees so that they lay piled up in twisted heaps, dead and forlorn. The road had been hacked through them, but it gave Daniel an eerie feeling nevertheless to see with what casual force Nature could destroy the growth of years.

There was one of these not far from Fort St. Clair, he recalled, and it was there, only thirteen days ago, that Colonel Strong's men had seen a large number of Indians. "Oh, well," he said to himself, half-aloud, "that don't mean they'll be there now!" He heard the echo of his own words with something of a shock. Thirteen days ago he could not have said such a thing, nor have felt so little fear.

That night, encamped at Fort St. Clair, he knew that Josiah and Ben were both alerted to all of Timothy's movements. But the big man lay quietly beside the fire, scarcely moving. Daniel was sure that the rendezvous was now past. Or, if that was not the case, then the other man—whoever he might be—wanted the supplies rather than the ponies.

CHAPTER NINE

There was a drizzle the next morning. It seemed like little enough rain, yet in a short time horses and men were soaking wet. The heat was intense and the air was steamy. Daniel was not sure whether the moisture he continually brushed from his brow was rain, or sweat, or both. Probably both.

They had had little breakfast. Josiah, when he had tried to buy some food for them at the fort, was told that the soldiers were in short supply themselves, and Ben, whose turn it had been to hunt the evening before, had had no luck. "Keep an eye out for some game," Josiah told Henry, "or Simon will have an empty kettle on the fire tonight."

Daniel's musket was ready to his hand. He thought it would be fine if he could shoot some game before Henry did, and his eyes shifted from left to right, searching the trees on either side of the road in the hope that he might spot something first. He doubted, however, if he would have the chance. Surely Simon's string, which was in the lead today, and Henry's, which was next, would have frightened off all the wild creatures before he came along.

Despite all this, when the shot rang out he was not expecting it, and his first thought was of the Indians. Yet he did not run, not even when there were cries from the front of the line, and the horses came to a halt. Amos called out to him, "What is it? Henry bag somethin' for dinner?"

But the cries held a note of distress, though Daniel could not make out the words. He ran out into the middle of the road and peered ahead. Someone was lying on the ground! It was Simon!

Amos saw the prone figure at the same moment. "Drive your hosses up to the others!" he called out. "Simon's hurt!"

It was only then that Daniel began to shake. Simon had been shot, perhaps killed. And who had done it? Where had the shot come from? His frantic glance darted in all directions. He wanted to get between two of his ponies for protection, but something within him forbade it. Still shaking, he drove his string forward, Amos following. Ben passed them at a run.

Josiah was bending over Simon when they came up. He raised his head, and instantly Daniel was reassured—he did not know why. "It ain't serious," Josiah said, "but he oughtn't to walk on it. Ben, you take the packsaddle off'n one of Simon's hosses, and rig up some blankets and things so's he'll ride comfortable. . . . Henry, you know where I keep the lint. And bring the water bottle, too."

He said to Amos, "Look in the woods, son, and see if you can find me some slippery elm bark. Best thing I know of for bullet wounds."

Daniel cried, "In the woods! But the Indians may still be there!"

"What Indians?" Josiah asked with a puzzled air. "Oh, you thought Simon had been shot by the Indians?" He chuckled. "No, he got shot by a feller named Simon."

At sight of Daniel's confused look, Simon said, sitting up, "Can't blame *this* on the Indians, I reckon. My own fault!"

"But how— You mean, you shot yourself?" Daniel asked.

"Sure thing. Thought I saw a buck in the woods—I *know* I saw a buck—and thought I'd beat Henry to it. Had my musket all loaded, too. Reached for my gun and didn't have the sense to step out in the road to fire it. The hoss behind nudged me, and the gun went off and blew a hole in my foot 'stead of in the buck. Now I'm lamed up and we ain't got no meat, neither!"

Amos came back with the news that he had not been able to locate any slippery elm in that section of the woods. "But I know where there is some," he added. "Only a couple miles from here. I'll get it when we come to the place."

Simon was mounted on one of the pack-horses, and Timothy was given Simon's string to drive, but since Simon was riding the last of the ponies of the string, there was not much Timothy would be able to do that would go unobserved.

Josiah sent the others back to their places, and the line of pack-horses began to move again. "We'll have to leave Simon at Fort Hamilton," was the last thing Daniel heard Josiah say.

Daniel was glad that the horses were traveling light, for that meant they could make good time to Fort Hamilton and get medical help for Simon. There was only one pause on the way, and that was when Amos called out that they had reached the place where he knew there was slippery elm. He disappeared into the woods for a few minutes with an axe and returned with some of the inner bark, which he handed to his father.

"We'll take it to the fort. Might be they don't have any on hand," Josiah said. "No time now to boil it and mash it and make it into a poultice. But there's nothing better to heal a wound that I know of."

Fort Hamilton, when they reached it, was seething with activity. Josiah went at once to get the help of the surgeon's mate for Simon, while Ben and Henry helped the wounded man through the gate. Amos craned his neck to stare inside the double line of pickets. "Looks like the whole two hunnerd soldiers is out and busy at somethin'. Never did see this place so bustlin' in all the times I been here. I wonder why?"

Daniel said, "They're none of 'em smilin'. Mebbe they've had bad news."

Amos chuckled. "Did you ever see a soldier workin' and smilin' at the same time, Dan'l? Mebbe they're expectin' a visit from Old Toney. I hear he hands out floggin's if there's so much as a piece of paper on the parade ground. Everything has to be neat and orderly, or he wants to know why."

But Daniel shook his head. These men were not going about their duties as if they were chores unwillingly performed. There was an urgency about them that bespoke something more important—something serious, or even dangerous.

They had to wait quite a while before Ben and Henry came out again. "Well, he's goin' to be as comfortable as a man can be with a hole in his foot," Ben said with satisfaction.

"Did they get the bullet out?" Amos asked.

"They sure did, and not a whimper out'n him. He bit his lip till the blood ran, and the sweat rolled off'n him like rain, but all he did was grunt a little once. Brave as an Indian."

Daniel noticed that Josiah was not with them. "Is Mr. Gregg stayin' with him a while?"

Ben sobered. "No, he's stopped to talk with Major Cass.

Seems there've been reports comin' in all afternoon of Indians in the neighborhood. Some says there's only a little band; others says there's a hunnerd of 'em at least. Major Cass don't know what to believe, but he does believe in bein' ready for 'em."

Amos said quickly, "What about the folks? Shouldn't we—"

"Oh, your pa'll push on to the farm, no doubt of it. But he wants to find out everything he can before we go." He sighed a little. "Timothy!" he called out. "Put that packsaddle back on the hoss Simon rode, and tie up the blankets the way they was. We'll be headin' out in a few minutes now."

Timothy came forward a little. "You mean to say we're goin' on when there's Indians on the rampage around here? It'll be dark afore you know it! Why don't we make camp here, where we'd have the fort at our back if we needed it?"

"Because Josiah wants to see to his family, that's why! Now, git movin'!"

Timothy's face was black with rage, and he muttered something under his breath, but with Ben watching him, he went about his business. In a few minutes, Josiah joined them. His strong face wore a frown of concentration.

"You men all got your muskets ready and loaded?" he asked. "Plenty of powder and shot to hand? Ben, I'll take the van, as usual. Timothy next, Henry next, then Dan'l and Amos, and you. I want every one of you to keep your eyes skinned for anythin' out of the ordinary along the road. I'd not think much of a scare like this if one man had had a fright and run to tell about it. But when three-four folks from different parts have the same kind of scare, there must be somethin' to it."

He walked to the head of the file of pack-horses, his gun at the ready, and gave the signal to march.

They passed the lovely prairie where the soldiers were wont to do their haying, but there were none there today. The weather had cleared and the late afternoon sun turned the grasses to brilliant green and gold. The long pond was visible beyond the meadow, and on their right the Big Miami River threw sparkles of light from the westering sun.

When they had crossed Pleasant Run they came to the little lane that led to the Gregg homestead. It was really dark in the woods, although there was still plenty of light in the open spaces. Daniel could feel the extra tension which came over the others. They were ready for anything, as he was.

This time is was Polly who saw them first. She was driving in one last unwilling cow from the woods, and let out a high shriek of welcome when she spied her father in the lead of the train.

"Pa!" she cried, running to greet him. "Ma *said* you'd get here, and we've been fixin' in case you did!" Her eyes swept down the line as more and more of the pack-horse train came into view. "Where's Simon?" she asked suddenly.

"We had to leave him at Fort Hamilton. He tride to shoot a buck so fast he tripped and shot himself! In the foot," he added quickly, so she wouldn't be too distressed. "The bullet's out and he's restin' comfortable. Only now we're one man short." He cocked his head and looked at her, then said with a chuckle, "If only you was a boy, and half as good as Dan'l, I'd take you along in Simon's stead."

She tossed her head and the tawny braids flounced. "Oh, no, you wouldn't!" she said pertly. " 'Cause then who'd do all the farm chores that I do?"

He chuckled again, and put his arm around her shoulders.

When they crossed Pleasant Run it was really dark in the woods.

"Not Ethan and Judah! Not those two rascals! And I reckon Sabrina's a mite small for milkin' cows, so mebbe I'll have to leave you here anyhow."

By this time they were within sight of the clearing, and the boys came running. Polly turned to Daniel. "If you'll help hold the cows," she said, "I'll get the milkin' done in a hurry. I'm late, but that's because I was helpin' Ma cook and bake."

"As soon as I've turned the hosses out," he promised her. Amos was already stacking the packsaddles and hobbling his string, his movements faster than usual, for he knew he would be needed for other farm chores.

That night, as they sat around the fire after a good meal of smoked venison ham, garden sass from the truck patch, and mush-and-milk, the talk turned to the future.

"When this war's over, and folks can work their farms peaceful," Ben said, "I'm goin' to open a store. Without the Indians to bother 'em, folks will be comin' to the Territory from all over. The land will get taken up, and then there'll be a cryin' need for all the things a storekeeper carries and a farmer ain't got."

"That'll take a while, Ben," Josiah said. "What you goin' to do in the meantime?"

"Likely I'll get me a couple ponies and do tradin'," Ben replied.

Josiah nodded. "That's a good way to get started," he admitted. "Then, when you have your store, you'll have customers that know your goods, and know you, too." He turned to Henry. "What do you aim to do?"

Henry looked surprised. "I thought you knew I was planning to teach," he said. "When I first came out, I had planned to farm and do a little teaching on the side. Now I'm pretty sure I'll teach, and do a little farming on the side."

Josiah frowned a little. "Folks are livin' too far apart to start a school hereabouts for a long time," he warned Henry.

"I wasn't thinking of this particular area," Henry said. "But there's Cincinnati. And Columbia. I rather incline to Columbia, where John Reily has been teaching. Though he gave up his school this past April, he may start it again. Or perhaps I could take over his pupils."

He raised his head and smiled confidently. "One thing is sure—the more developed this country becomes, the more need there will be for education. . . . Take these two lads." He nodded toward Amos and Daniel. "As long as this part of the world is so little inhabited, they've small need of a knowledge of reading and writing and figuring. But once the settlements begin to grow—as they will grow when peace comes—then people will want schooling." He turned suddenly toward Daniel. "Can you read?" he asked.

Daniel flushed. "I was never learned," he said quickly. "My ma taught me some of my letters, but when we come to the Territory Pa was too busy in the daytime and too tired at night to do much teachin'. But he'd take a stick sometimes and draw the letters for me in the ashes, or on the ground. I reckon I still know 'em all. . . . 'Course the Worders, where I lived, didn't read nor write."

Henry nodded. "And when times get better, and the Worders make something of their farm—if they do—they may be at the mercy of any skinflint who tries to cheat them."

Timothy snorted. "Readin' and writin' don't keep folks from bein' cheated!"

"No," Henry said, "but at least they've had some mental discipline and are not dependent upon others to make out their contracts and bills of sale."

Josiah turned to Amos. "I know what you want to do," he said with a smile. "Or I think I do."

Amos said, "That's right. I'm goin' to buy me some of that land north of Fort Hamilton and have my own farm when I'm a man grown. But first, I think I'll go along with Ben for a while. That way I'll get to see more of the country, and mebbe find me an even better spot. Besides, I'll earn money that way to buy the land."

"And you, Dan'l?" Mrs. Gregg asked. He was sitting beside her.

Daniel sighed. "I'd sooner work on a farm and earn money that way," he said. "But you don't make enough doin' that, so I reckon I'd better find somethin' I can do. Mebbe I could learn a trade in Cincinnati so's to earn enough that way."

"And you, Timothy?" The small pig eyes were turned briefly upon Josiah. Once the food had disappeared, Timothy had shown little interest in the conversation. "What do you want to do?"

"Go to sleep," Timothy grunted rudely, and lay down beside the fire.

"Time for all of us to get to bed," Mrs. Gregg said. She picked up Sabrina. The sleeping child was limp in her arms, its head rolling to one side. Ethan and Judah were stifling yawns. This talk had been as boring to them as it had been to Timothy, Daniel could see. But Polly's eyes were bright with excitement.

He turned to her as she rose to go. "If you were a man, what would you like to do?" he asked. Somehow, he sensed that these thoughts had been flying through her mind.

"Oh, so many things!" she cried. "I'd like to fight with Gen'l Wayne! Or go west, explorin'—there's so much to see and so many places nobody has seen yet—no white folks, I mean. Or travel to the east and see the big cities, like Philadelphia or Boston." Suddenly she drooped a little. "But I reckon I'll just stay here and do the things a woman does, no matter where she is."

"Let that be your consolation," Henry said, smiling.

"Yes," she agreed. Then she added with suppressed vehemence, "Only I just wish *somethin'* excitin' would happen *sometime!*"

CHAPTER TEN

Daniel opened his eyes sleepily. It was still dark, but there was a faint suggestion of grayness to herald the dawn. He frowned a little, wondering why he had wakened so early.

A sudden loud report startled him. Something whistled past his ear. He was on his feet with one bound. "Indians!" he shouted at the top of his lungs. On the echo of his shout came the long ululating yell of savages in the cover of the woods.

The others who had been sleeping about the fire were on their feet almost as soon as he was. "The hosses!" roared Josiah. "Git the hosses!"

Daniel snatched up his musket and ran toward the place where he had loosed his string the previous night. The horses had been hobbled, as always, and he felt sure they could not have gone too far. But they were in the woods, where it was still completely dark, and the Indians were in the woods, too.

He saw, from the corner of his eye, the racing figures of Josiah, Ben, Henry, and Amos. There was another, smaller figure coming from the house, running on fleet feet. Polly!

A movement in the woods made him drop down behind a tree to fire. He heard a yell after his shot had sped toward the half-seen target, and hoped that he had hit one of the marauders. Henry, on his left, was firing coolly, and reloading and firing again with incredible speed.

Daniel forced himself to go forward toward the line of trees. The horses were in there. If he did not move quickly, the Indians would have stolen them all. He wanted, as he had wanted nothing else in his life, to be brave just this once. To find Josiah's horses, to help this man who had befriended him. But he did not know whether he could make his feet obey his will.

Several of the horses, frightened by the noise, now came running from the woods. Their hobbles had been removed, their bells silenced. Daniel and Amos caught them and turned them over to Polly to tie together securely. The animals were wild and rearing, and Daniel wondered if Polly could handle them, but she managed them easily. Polly could do many things.

There was no time to think. He and Amos ran back toward the woods again. The menfolk had disappeared, and he realized that they had entered the forest to stalk the attackers. A rifle barrel was thrust from the window of the cabin that fronted toward the woods, and Daniel knew that it was held steadily by Mrs. Gregg.

Two more horses came charging from the woods, urged on by Ben who was briefly glimpsed thwacking them on the rump. Daniel caught them, but found he could not hold them and his musket, too.

"Here, let me," Polly said at his side, taking one of the horses from him and starting to lead it back toward the house.

A swift, painted figure leaped from behind one of the trees nearby, and the rifle in the window spoke. The man fell to the ground.

"Good shot, Ma!" Polly shrieked. Her shift was torn, and her tawny hair flew in the wind. Daniel suddenly found himself laughing. He did not know why.

His laugh was cut short as another Indian, mounted on a

horse, swept from the woods. There hadn't been time for Mrs. Gregg to reload, Daniel knew. He tried to raise his own musket, but the horse to whose bridle he was clinging, reared and knocked the gun from his hands. The mounted Indian came straight at Polly. Without a second thought, Daniel rushed to put himself between them, but the Indian swerved and caught up the girl as if she had been made of thistledown. With one hand he held her struggling form while he guided the horse back to the forest.

Daniel threw himself on the back of the horse he was holding and raced after them. He had no gun, but he did not stop to think of that. He had nothing but his hunting knife and his anger.

The Indian was a skillful rider, but Daniel's horse was the faster. Besides, the other horse had to bear the weight of two. Daniel could see that Polly had not ceased struggling. He knew that if the Indian could free his bridle hand for a moment, he would strike her senseless.

Daniel shouted at the top of his lungs, "Let her go! Let her go!" He lay along the neck of his horse and kicked the animal with his heels. Every second counted now! His hand fumbled for his knife. He was not good at throwing a knife, but he would make a try.

The horses streaked through the woods in zigzag fashion. A fallen tree was jumped, quick turns made around heavy thickets. Daniel kept shouting, hoping that one of the others at the homestead might hear him. Yet he knew that this was a foolish hope. The clearing was far behind now.

Suddenly the Indian seemed to come to a decision. He pulled up sharply, turned about, and lifted his gun to take aim at

Daniel. The moment his hand was lifted from her, Polly slipped to the ground. She rolled into some bushes. Daniel had only time to see that much. He had his knife raised and, just before the Indian fired, he threw it.

The knife did not strike the Indian, but it glanced off his horse's rump so that the animal reared, and the bullet meant for Daniel sped harmlessly skyward. Instantly, seeing that his shot had missed the target, the Indian flung his tomahawk. Daniel, clinging to the neck of his horse, leaned far down on one side, almost sliding off. The tomahawk passed over his head with a hissing sound.

His thoughts were racing madly. The Indian must have a knife. He could come at Daniel with that. And Daniel had nothing but his bare hands. Without hesitation, he kicked his horse again and charged straight at the Indian.

Whether the Indian thought that such a move must mean Daniel had other weapons, the boy never knew. What mattered was that the ruse worked. With a swift movement, the Indian turned his horse and fled into the darkness of the forest.

For one exhilarating second, Daniel was tempted to follow. Without a weapon, he had forced an Indian to run from him! But Polly was struggling to her feet from the clump of bushes into which she had fallen. At any moment the Indian might return with some of his fellows. The only sensible thing to do was to retreat toward the farmhouse.

Daniel reached down his hand to Polly and she grasped it firmly. She put her bare foot against the horse's side and, with Daniel's strong pull, landed in front of him upon the horse. She was gasping.

"Turn to the right, Dan'l. It's a mite swampy—in there, and

the Indians—wouldn't be goin' that way. We can work around
—to the house. I know the way."

It was getting lighter, even in the woods, as they moved off
to the right. The ground soon grew boggy and the horse picked
its way with care. They could no longer hear any shots and
Polly, breathing easily now, laughed. "They've beat 'em off,"
she said with confidence.

It could mean just the opposite, as Daniel knew all too well.
But, strangely, he felt as certain as Polly that the Indians had
been repulsed. When they came to drier ground they spied a
number of the pack-horses ahead of them, huddled in a little
group.

Daniel slipped off his horse. "You stay here," he told Polly,
"and I'll catch 'em."

But the horses stood quietly, and when he got to them, he saw that they were tied together with a buffalo tug. "Look!" he cried. "We can lead 'em all in together!"

As they neared the farmhouse clearing, the welcome sound of voices greeted them. Josiah was shouting orders, Ben and Henry were running back toward the woods, and Amos was securely hobbling the horses that had been salvaged so far. When Daniel and Polly appeared there was a sudden silence, then a shout of relief.

"Dan'l's got her!" Josiah yelled, and the others came forward.

"Where'd you find her?"

"Did you kill the Indian?"

"How could you? We found your gun here!"

"Now, God be thanked!" This last was Josiah, as he lifted Polly from the horse and hugged her briefly. He held her off then to look at her. "Not hurt, are you, Polly? You've got a mort of scratches, I see, and mebbe a few bruises. But you're not hurt, are you?"

"No, Pa," she said. "But I might ha' been if Dan'l hadn't come after me. You never saw anythin' like the way he went for that Indian!" She beamed on Daniel who flushed happily.

For the first time he realized just what he had done. He had faced an Indian in uneven battle and had forced the Indian to flee! Best of all, he couldn't remember that he had been scared at all while it was happening!

"Dan'l went after the Indian?" That was Amos, his friend. But it was said kindly. "And without his gun?"

Daniel said, still wondering at his own courage, "I was so

mad when I saw him lightin' out with Polly that I didn't stop to git afeared."

Mrs. Gregg was with them by this time, Sabrina in her arms, and Ethan and Judah clinging to her skirts. This was their first Indian raid and Daniel, with real understanding of how they felt, smiled at them.

"Polly, you're a sight," her mother said, smiling. "Best go in now and put your clothing to rights. And comb your hair."

"But, Ma, there's still some ponies to find. If the Indians haven't run 'em off."

For the first time, Josiah really noticed the horses that Daniel was still holding. "Where'd you git all those?" he marveled. Then, his eyes lighting on the buffalo tug, he cried, "Why, the Indians had them all rounded up and ready to go! With what we've found so far, that means there's only four to find."

"I'll help!" Polly cried, but her mother shooed her firmly into the house.

"You'll make yourself neat first," Daniel heard her say, as they disappeared through the doorway, "and then you'll help me fix breakfast for the men."

"Mmm, breakfast!" Josiah said with a sigh of content. "Come on, Dan'l, we'll git in the firewood, and the others can bring in the ponies." He headed around the house toward the log pile.

A fat face with heavy jowls and small pig-eyes rose from behind the pile of wood. It was pale and the jowls were shaking with fear. "Are—are they gone?" Timothy croaked.

Josiah stopped in his tracks. "So that's where you were!" he growled. "We looked for you—thought mebbe the Indians had got you, but I reckon they've more sense than to want a scalp like yours!" His voice rose suddenly to a bellow, and he strode forward threateningly. "A coward, are you? Hidin' when there's danger! Well, I've no use for the likes of you. I'll sooner go it alone than depend on a spineless critter that runs at the first whoop of danger."

He pulled out his purse. "Here's your pay! You can walk back to Fort Hamilton, or you can walk on to Fort Washington and Cincinnati; but wherever you go, keep out of *my* way!" He thrust a few coins at the man and when Timothy reached for them, jerked him out of the woodpile by the tail of his shirt. "Now, git goin' afore I boot you out of here!"

For a moment Timothy straightened, and his mouth twisted in a snarl. "You hired me for the trip. You got to keep me," he said. "You'll be sorry if you don't—"

Then Josiah got really angry. "Threaten me, will you?" he shouted. "And with what? More hosses breakin' loose? More sore backs on the ones that's left?" He took a step toward the other man, and Timothy cringed away from him. "It begins to look like you *did* let those hosses get away a-purpose. Had you sold 'em to somebody, mebbe? Somebody you met in the woods that night?"

Timothy turned without an answer, and half ran, half shambled around the house and down the lane toward the road. He cowered as he went, and his head twisted from side to side, as if he saw an Indian behind every bush and tree. Josiah watched him for a moment, then turned to Daniel.

"Looks like you were right about him," he said. "I reckon we'll never know for sure *who* he met that night." Then he added mildly, "Well, Ma'll be wonderin' why we don't bring in the firewood," and picked up an armload.

Daniel followed suit. He could well understand how furious Josiah must be. Yet it was strange that he had seemed more angered by Timothy's hiding during the Indian raid than he had been by the loss of the horses in the man's string on the previous trip.

He wanted desperately to ask Josiah something, but he didn't quite dare. Why had Josiah been so harsh to Timothy for his cowardice and so lenient to Daniel for his? The answer came to him after a few moments. Daniel had been fearful—and not just during the Indian attack, but all the time—yet he had made himself do the things he was afraid to do. He had conquered his fear at last, while Timothy had let fear conquer him.

There was leftover venison and fresh johnnycake for breakfast, and the men ate heartily. All but one of the horses had been recovered, thanks to Daniel's discovery of the ones the Indians had tied together for driving away.

"Mebbe the one that's missin' is the one the Indian was ridin'," Amos suggested.

"That wasn't one of ours," Daniel said with conviction. "I mean, one of yours."

But Josiah put his hand on the lad's shoulder. "It's 'ours', son," he said in his deep voice. "After what you did this morning, you can have anythin' we have. Ain't it so, Ma?"

"It certainly is," she said, nodding with emphasis. "This is your home, Dan'l, whenever you want it to be."

"And don't forget it!" Josiah boomed.

Daniel, looking about the circle of faces, thought how rich he had become in this short while. He had a job, he was earning money, he was seeing the world. Better still, he had friends. And now, best of all, he was to have a family. His eyes filled with tears, and he got up abruptly.

"I reckon I'd better go see if I can find my knife afore we leave," he said. "I know just about where I threw it, so it ought to be there still."

Without even thinking of danger from lurking Indians, Daniel walked toward the woods.

THE AUTHOR

CATEAU DE LEEUW lived in Ohio until her family moved to Plainfield, New Jersey, when she was ten years old. After graduating from high school, she studied portrait painting at the Metropolitan School of Art and the Art Students' League in New York. Several years later she opened her own studio.

Her career as an author began by chance when she collaborated with her sister Adele on short stories for magazines. "This was a good thing," she says, "because there was a depression and portrait commissions were scarcer than dinosaur eggs." Her first book, published in 1943, has been followed by more than twenty others—fiction and nonfiction, some for adults, but most of them for young people.

Miss De Leeuw has many hobbies: playing the organ, fencing, jewelry-making, needle-point, and weaving. No wonder she can say that she is *never* bored.